MARKED

MEASHA STONE

Copyright © 2024 by Black Heart Publications and Measha Stone

All rights reserved.

No part of this book may be reproduced in any form or by any electronic or mechanical means, including photocopying, recording, or by any informational storage and retrieval system without permission in writing from the publisher, except for the use of brief quotations in a book review.

The author and publisher do not give permission for any part of this book to be used to create, feed, or refine artificial intelligence models for any any purpose.

Marked

Cover Design by Deranged Doctor Design

Content Editing by Hart to Heart Edits

Line Editing by Fairy Plot Mother

Published by Black Heart Publications, LLC

Stone, Measha

WARNING

Marked is a dark, twisted, psychological thriller involving those that have killed and those that will be killed. Possible triggers are: non-consent activities, cutting, blood play, and overall bad things happening to good people, who then do bad things to bad people. If you find any of these things to be triggering or unappealing, please turn back now.

To everyone else...you've been warned.

ONE

Zack

A speck of blood marks my knuckles.

After licking my thumb, I wipe the spot clean, then climb out of my car. Even with my sunglasses on, the sun glaring down on me from high in the sky is blinding.

Rounding the back of my car, I tap on the trunk. "We have some time. How about a cup of coffee?"

A grumble and a thud respond. I leave it behind, hopping up onto the curb and heading for the door.

Inside the coffee shop, the windows have a heavy tint, not allowing much of the sunlight to creep inside.

I tuck the arm of my sunglasses into the front of my black T-shirt as I step into the short line at the cashier.

We're over an hour outside of Chicago, past the suburbs, nestled deep into the corn crops and soybeans of the Midwest. But even way out here, the coffee chains have made a home.

I can see the appeal of a town like this. A twenty-minute drive will bring you to all the modern conveniences, but you'll still have the simplicity of a small-town community.

Not that I'd ever consider settling down in one spot for too long.

Too much work to do all over the country.

Fuck, the world. It's a dark place, and a man like me thrives in th darkness.

"Sorry." A soft voice comes after a shoulder bumps into mine.

I turn, finding the offending shoulder attached to a woman. A blonde-haired beauty with soft caramel eyes, and they're focused on me.

"Sorry," she mutters again, her eyes fleeing my gaze as soon as they land.

"Not a problem," I say, watching her scurry to the corner of the coffee shop with her covered paper cup. She tucks herself into the booth, and pulls a paperback from her bag before moving it to the seat across from her.

Not interested in company.

Message received.

I move up in the line, still watching her as she turns the pages of her book to find her last page.

She sips her drink, licking away a bit of foam that escaped through the lid and smeared across her bottom lip. The name 'Harley' is scribbled on the side of her cup. An ID badge has slipped out of her bag, dangling from a lanyard tucked inside. Her full name is Harley Turner, and she's a teacher at the local elementary school.

As though she can feel my attention, she glances up from her book just enough to survey the room. I keep my stance loose, my attention on a spot where I can see her in my peripheral vision.

When her eyes land on me, they linger.

Heat builds just below my skin the longer she stares. I turn a little more in her direction, making it look as though I'm checking out the mugs on the wall not far to her right.

She still stares.

I almost smile.

But I don't want her to know that I see her.

I want her to have herself a long look. I want her to feel me in the room before I approach her.

If I approach her.

I'm on a deadline.

No time for flirtation today.

"Can I help you, sir?" the cashier calls to me. My turn.

"A small coffee, cream and sugar." I hand over a few bills to cover it. No credit cards. No debit cards. Nothing that can be traced to me.

Even my fingerprints on that bill won't get anyone anywhere.

I move over to the waiting area for my coffee, still keeping my eyes on the book beauty in the corner. She's back to reading.

Her face tenses. She winces, and pulls her hand from the book. She's given herself a paper cut.

Her middle finger disappears into her mouth, leaving a small smudge of blood just below her bottom lip. It's a tiny amount. I doubt anyone around her sees it. But I've got an eye for blood. Seeing every bit of it helps when cleaning it up.

She puts her book down with a sigh, and takes another sip of her drink. Her eyes line up with mine again, and this time she doesn't dart them away.

There's something in her gaze, something familiar. She's fearful, but she's forcing herself not to hide.

She's strong.

But I doubt she can see it.

A moment goes by, then another. We're just staring at each other. I won't look away first. I want to see how long I can hold her attention.

Fear is an aphrodisiac. People may not like to admit it, but it's the truth. And truth is what I'm all about.

The scent of fear is strong, and gets stronger the longer she stares into my eyes.

Slowly, I arch my eyebrow, tilting my head in her direction.

A dare.

Will she come to me, or will she dive back into her book?

The pull between us increases the longer this little standoff of ours continues. Like two magnets inching closer and closer, until the force of attraction is too strong to be fought and they smash together.

"Connor." The barista calls out the name I've chosen for this job.

The blonde beauty breaks eye contact to look at the barista. When she swings her eyes back to me, the fear is gone.

I give her a hint of a smile.

She thinks she's safe now.

I grab my coffee from the counter.

What a curious little bird.

I glance back at her as I head to the door. Her eyes dart to her book.

Hmmm. She's watching me.

I push my sunglasses back on and head back to my car, stopping at the trunk.

Popping it open, I hold it to keep it from opening all the way. No need to give the neighbors a full view of my work.

"It's a hot day. Hope you're keeping cool back here." I take a casual sip of my coffee before looking down at him. Sweat mingles with the dried blood around the duct tape keeping his mouth shut.

Keeping the lid as closed as possible while holding my coffee, I reach inside and rip the tape off. Little droplets of fresh blood appear around his mouth.

Duct tape is not kind to the skin.

"How well do you know the people in this town?"

"Where are we?" He tries to get up, but with his hands bound to his feet, it's not so easy.

I tilt my head. "Think, asshole. I told you we're retracing your steps. We're about ten minutes from your secret playground." I take another sip. Shit, this coffee is good. I might need to make a second trip for another cup.

"I don't know. I don't hang out in town." He brushes his cheek against his shoulder, wiping away some of the blood and sweat, smearing more dirt onto his shirt.

"Didn't think so." I sigh. "Shame."

"Please! Just fucking let me go. Let me up. If you need information, I can get it for you, but you gotta let me out of this." He tugs on his binds.

I close the trunk a little more.

The desperation is just pathetic at this point. He's begged so much in the last day, I'm a little bored with it.

I don't take on any job unless I know, without a doubt, the fucker has it coming.

And this fucker has everything coming to him.

"Jessica was in your trunk for how long?" I tilt my head a little. "The report was vague."

He pales.

"Please." His eyes narrow. I think he's trying not to cry. Doesn't matter. As soon as we get started with his actual punishment, he'll be sobbing like the pussy he is.

"Tell me." I lift a shoulder. "Let's see if you're starting to learn how to be trustworthy."

He sniffs. "Five hours, I think."

I check my watch. A gift from the last commander I served under in the Marines. It's one of those sport kinds that takes one hell of a beating and doesn't die.

"Looks like you have another hour." He starts to wiggle around, but no one's ever gotten out of one of my hog ties. He won't be the first.

I slam the trunk, then take my coffee to the front seat of my car.

With the added fuel from the fresh cup of coffee, I can finish the drive to Mr. Carpenter's little playground. The place where he enjoyed himself two years ago.

There's a price of admission for every party, even if it comes years later.

I couldn't stop the horror he'd brought to Jessica Hamilton, but I can bring her justice now.

An eye for an eye.

And when I'm done with him, every second of terror he made that young woman live through will have been revisited upon him.

As I pull away from the coffee shop, I notice Harley stepping outside, the sun hitting her face. She tilts her head back, letting the sun bathe her skin as she slides on a pair of sunglasses.

I'll be done with Mr. Carpenter by morning.

And then, Harley Turner will get my full attention.

A tingle of excitement trails up my spine. I woke up today like it was any other ordinary day of work. But now, thanks to Harley, it looks like there's going to be some fun in my life.

Until tomorrow, Harley.

Until tomorrow.

TWO

Harley

"Hey, Harley," Johnny greets me as I empty Mom's grocery cart onto the checkout conveyor belt.

"Hey, Johnny." I have to bend into the cart to get the last bit, a dozen eggs, and a package of strawberries.

"Your mom with you?" Johnny asks, starting to scan Mom's weeks' worth of groceries.

Glancing over the rack of magazines and recipe books, I search for my mother. As soon as we'd gotten in line, she'd dashed off for one more thing.

"Yeah. She's coming." I point to her walking toward us with a package of hot dogs. She hates hot dogs, and I've never liked them. But they were a staple in our house up until I was thirteen.

"I almost forgot!" She waves the package at me as she side steps through the people behind us and drops it on the conveyer belt.

"Did you need buns?" Johnny points to the package.

I shake my head.

"No. Thanks." I pull the cart through the checkout lane and start loading the bags into it.

"Harley." Mom wiggles her fingers to get my attention. "Hun, can you hand me my wallet; it's in my purse." She points to the black handbag in the cart.

I dig through it, find the small wallet, and go to hand it to her.

"Can you grab my debit card for me?" She opens her palm.

I open the well-worn, leather, folded-up wallet. I freeze, just for a moment, before flipping past the wallet-sized photographs, all of them of Quinn, and finding her debit card.

I wait for her to slide the card through the machine and hand it back to me, keeping her wallet closed and not giving into the temptation to flip through the photographs. There are more of them now.

When Mom hands the debit card back to me, I shove it in her wallet and throw it back in the bag.

"What's wrong?" she asks me, after finishing with Johnny.

"Nothing," I say, moving out of the way as she pushes the cart toward me. "Want me to push?" I offer.

"Yes. Please." She releases the cart and steps to the side. I grab ahold of it before it rolls off into the vending machine of scratch-off lottery tickets.

"Do you want to stop at the library on the way home?" I ask.

"No. I'm tired." She sighs as we walk through the electronic doors and into the parking lot.

"All right." I follow her to my car and open her door for her before unloading her groceries into my trunk.

It's hot today. The humidity has my hair frizzing and sticking to my neck.

I close the trunk of my well-used Toyota Camry and freeze.

A man.

A *specific* man stands across the parking lot, in front of a car, staring at me.

It's the same man from the coffee shop yesterday afternoon.

He has sunglasses on this time, but his build is the same. Muscular, broad, like he puts a lot of effort into his physique. His jaw line squeezes when I don't move.

Just like yesterday, the same dark brown eyebrow arches over his left eye. He's challenging me, I think. He definitely wants something.

"Harley, what's wrong?" Mom calls from her opened window. "Hun, you okay?"

"Yeah. I'm fine, Mom." I break eye contact with him and push the cart to the return.

When I head back, I look for him, but he's not there. His car is, but he's gone.

I shake my head. He wasn't here for me. It's a grocery store. He's getting groceries. That's all.

But my skin tingles, like he's still watching me. Turning around and then around again, I search the lot and the store entrance for any sign of him, but come up empty.

He's not watching me.

I close my eyes and take a deep breath, pushing my abdomen out. Repeating this three times, I get my heart to slow, my brain to mellow.

He's not here for me.

No one is here for me.

"Harley?" Mom leans across the console to look up at me through my window. "Hun, you sure you're all right?"

"Sorry," I say once I'm inside the car, pulling on my seatbelt. "I thought I saw someone I knew."

"Oh, who? Someone from work?" She pulls her bag into her lap, slips her wallet out, and works the zipper closed.

"No one." I reverse out of my spot and head towards her house.

"You thought you saw no one?" She chuckles and looks out her window as I drive. "I think this heat's getting to you."

She turns the radio on and up, a signal that she doesn't want to talk. In her lap, she's gripping her wallet with both hands. Her thumb is tucked inside, between the pictures.

Deep breath.

Clear the mind.

Slow the breathing.

Once we're at her house, she goes inside and leaves the front screen door propped open for me so I can bring in the bags. It takes three trips, but I get everything inside and brought to the kitchen, then I close the front door.

"You'll stay for dinner, right, hun?" She opens the fridge, putting away the lettuce and cheese.

"Oh. No, Mom. Thanks, but I have some stuff to do tonight." I bring the boxed rice to the pantry. I haven't lived inside these walls in seven years, but everything is exactly the same. Once I'm here, sometimes it feels like I never left.

Like I'll never get away.

"What do you have to do?" She turns from the fridge with a frown. Her hair, once shoulder length with thick curls and colored a warm chestnut blonde, is now cropped just below her ears and has faded to a mixture of dirty blonde and gray. Her crystal blue eyes stand out against the dull coloring of her hair.

"Just things." I lift a shoulder. It's summer, and my last day of classes was two weeks ago. I won't have anything work related to keep me busy for another six weeks.

"Do you have a date?" Her voice tilts upward, like she's hopeful that I do. But we've danced to this tune before.

"No, Mom. I just have a few things I want to get done around the apartment. I'm thinking of hosting a book club this month." I've thought about it a lot of times. A group of women, my age, talking about our latest read over a bottle of wine, maybe a cheese board.

It sounds so normal.

So casual.

So terrifying.

"Oh? What book?" She shuts the fridge and leans back against the counter's edge.

"I'm not sure yet. I was thinking of talking to the librarians and seeing if they have a suggestion, or going on the internet. I know there are a lot of groups online." And I've been too chickenshit to even join those.

"Well, you can do that after dinner." She waves a hand through the air, as though to shove the idea of my existance outside this house away.

The grandfather clock in the living room chimes. I jump at the sudden, deep sound of it, and she shakes her head at me.

"Just the clock, Harley," she says. "We'll go through those papers I told you about, and then I'll get dinner on."

"Mom. Thanks, but I really can't tonight." I won't stay. "I'll come over Thursday. We can go to the diner you like for dinner."

"We can do that, too." She picks up a bag of lettuce and tosses it in the fridge. "It's a rough week, honey, for both of us. Shutting ourselves in won't make it any easier."

I let loose a slow breath. She's right. As hard as it is for me, it must be even worse for her. Only by her choice am I here today. I need to be grateful, sympathetic.

"It is." I nod. "What is the paperwork you wanted me to take a look at? Is it your retirement package?" Mom retired last year. It's not that she's too old to keep working, the woman has a mind as sharp as a filet knife. But she's taught second grade for twenty-five years. She'd had enough.

"No. I went through that already. I got a call from your father's work." She redirects the conversation so quickly; it takes me a second to rejoin her.

"The plastics plant? I thought they went out of business years ago." They'd laid him and half his team off when he was first diagnosed, taking away not only his income, but his health insurance. Three years after he passed away from lung cancer, the plant had been shut down.

I was happy when I heard on the news that the company had gone out of business and the owner had declared bankruptcy. He'd lost everything to a competitor who'd eaten up the market.

No one deserved it more than that man.

A year later, when it was revealed that his wife had left him and he'd eaten a bullet, I smiled. I'd even gone to his grave after his funeral and danced.

The fucker.

A bullet was too easy for him, he should have been given a slow and painful death. Like Dad.

"They did shut down, but the company was actually purchased by someone. They called to tell me there was a small pension your father never mentioned. He would be sixty-five now if he hadn't died, so they are offering to pay it out."

"Oh. That's good, right? You'll get that now, right?" I loosen my grip on the chair. More income will do her good. Her own pension is enough for her to live on, and she'd been good at saving over the years. But any added cushion will help ease her mind. And this time of year, anything that helps her relax is helpful.

"It's not much, but yes. I get it." She finishes putting the rest of the vegetables away. "I'll get the paperwork." She disappears into her bedroom that's just off the living room, and when she returns, she's carrying a two-inch, three-ring binder.

"They sent all that?" I point to the thick stack of paperwork.

"No, but I put what they sent in here." It thunks as it hits the kitchen table, and she flips open the cover. "Everything for your dad is in here." She fingers the tabs on the side of the pages until she finds the one labeled 'Pension.'

She hands me the letter first, while working the stapled packet from the rings. At a quick glance, it seems all straightforward.

"Is there a direct deposit form in there?" I point to the packet she's holding.

"Yes." She flips through and finds it.

"All right. You need to fill that out, so the money just goes straight to your bank account. Unless you want a paper check? But it looks like there's a fee for that."

"A fee for a real check? Is that legal?" She sinks down into one of the kitchen chairs and I do the same.

"I'm not sure. I doubt they'd do it if they couldn't." I flip through the rest of the packet. Standard information, nothing out of the ordinary. "Mom. It's almost a thousand dollars a month." I stop at the last page with the calculations on it.

"Well, Dad was in his forties when they let him go. He'd worked there for almost twenty years." She takes the packet back, running her fingers over the page. "It would have been nice to know about this back then, though. I could have cashed it in."

She blinks away tears and looks away from me while she wipes her hand across her eyes.

"It would have helped with the medical costs and his funeral. And then..." She shakes her head, not finishing the thought. "Maybe things could have been different."

It would have helped with the burial expenses for Quinn, too.

My stomach clenches.

"Well, you'll have it now. But you should do the direct deposit."

She nods. "Yes. Of course. Let me get my checkbook so I can fill it out. You have a scanner thingy at home, right? Can you take it and send it for me?" She's already out of the kitchen when she finishes her question.

"Sure," I say to the empty room, checking that the form can be emailed.

I glance over at the binder and pull it toward me. Dad's been gone for twelve years now; why does she still have all this?

I tab through each category; Medical, Funeral, Credit Cards, Blackwood, Pension.

Blackwood? What the hell is that?

"Here we go." She breezes back in with her checkbook and pen in hand. Moving the binder away from me, she sits back down and fills out the form in silence. I eye the binder.

"Dad didn't have life insurance?" I ask, noticing there's no tab for it.

She looks up after scribbling her signature on the form. "Hmm?"

"You have nothing for life insurance." I point to the binder.

"Oh, it's there." She reaches over and closes the binder, pushing the form at me. "You'll send it tonight?"

"Yep." I push my chair back, ready to get home. There're too many memories here of a past I can't outrun.

"You're not staying for dinner?" She frowns.

I roll my shoulders back and look her in the eyes.

Be firm.

Be direct.

"No, Mom. But thanks for the offer."

"But I'm making macaroni and cheese with hot dogs." She points to the package sitting on the counter.

"Mom." I soften my tone. "I don't like hot dogs."

Her eyes pierce me for a long moment. "Yes, you do. You used to beg me to make them all the time."

"No, Mom." I shake my head. "That wasn't me." I almost whisper the last bit.

We don't directly address the elephant that lives in this house. It's a delicate dance of scooting around without disturbing it, for fear of the thick tusks goring us in the ass.

The silence lengthens, gets heavier as she continues to stare at me. I pick up the cans of black beans and bring them to the pantry, placing them next to the Great Northern beans. She likes things grouped by category in her pantry.

"Oh. That's right." She grabs the hot dogs and opens the fridge, ready to chuck them inside.

"Mom, wait." I stop her, pushing the elephant further out of the room. "Dinner sounds good, actually. It's been a long time since I've tried macaroni and cheese with hot dogs. I bet it's better than I remember." I put on a smile, hoping it looks genuine and warm.

She's been through so much, had so much taken from her. It won't hurt me to give her this. It's just dinner after all.

She gave up so much for me.

It's the least I can do.

"Great. I'll get them on the stove." She practically beams with joy, and closes the fridge.

I sit back in my chair, watching Mom cook my sister's favorite meal. I'll hate it, just as much I did when we were little. But my mother did the unthinkable for me. I can shovel this meal down if it makes her happy.

The elephant disappears, and it's just the two of us now.

As it's been since Quinn's murder.

THREE

Harley

Even after eleven years, I still feel it to my bones. The blame, the guilt, the regret. It's soaked into my soul and there's no getting it out.

I hear the whispers.

"She's the one."

"Poor Quinn."

"Poor Mrs. Turner. Can you imagine it?"

And I step deeper into the darkness. I'm warm there.

I'm sheltered from the blotchy memories. I'm told they are too horrific for my mind to allow me access. Dissociative Amnesia. The selective variety, the doctors explained.

All I have are jumbled up images that make no sense, and get distorted when I try to focus on them. My memory may come back, or it may not, but the important thing was to stop trying to force it.

So, for eleven years, I've had days cut out of my memory. In the gap is where I settle my mind. Where it's dark, and quiet, and only I can fit.

"What can I get you, Harley? Your usual?" Samantha asks

from behind the register. I've known her since we were in elementary school together. She was Quinn's best friend up until seventh grade.

She probably blames me.

If I knew the whole story, maybe I would too.

Quinn was a ray of sunshine. She shone so brightly; it pushed me into the shadows. Why should I have been the one who was chosen? It's this question that keeps me mindful. I need to be worthy of the life given.

"Yes, please." I pull out my phone, swiping open the app to pay for my Grande caramel latte. Same coffee, same seat at the coffee house, same time each day. Teaching fourth grade has taught me how important routine is to keep an organized life.

My mind may dance with chaos in the darkness, but I have to live out here in the light.

"We'll have it ready for you in a just a minute." She smiles, already looking at the customer behind me.

I find my usual seat. A small booth in the back corner. I'm able to see the front door from here. It's important to always be able to see the door. That way I can tell who's coming at me.

The book I'm reading is buried at the bottom of my bag. By the time I dig it out and lay it on the table, the barista calls my name.

I hurry to the counter to grab it, but when I get there, there's only a small cup with the name 'Zack' scribbled on the side.

Thinking I'm hearing things today, I sit back down and wait. But my name isn't called, as another drink is put out on the counter. The only other person standing nearby takes it and walks out of the shop. I glance over at the workers; they're wiping things down, chatting. No one's making another drink.

I sigh and head to the counter to check the cup again.

It hasn't changed. It still reads Zack.

"Hi. I heard you call my name, but I don't see my drink." I wave slightly at Jacob who's wiping down the steamer.

He looks over at the counter, then picks up the drink.

"He must have taken yours." He points to the window. "He's sitting out there. I'll make you a new one."

I twist to see who has my drink. My stomach sinks.

It's him.

The same man from the shop two days ago. From the grocery store yesterday.

He's looking at me through the window, sipping my coffee. I can't see his eyes; his sunglasses are on. But his eyebrow arches again, and he leans back in the chair like he's ready to wait for me as long as it takes.

It's not normal to feel someone beckoning to you when they aren't making any gestures or sounds. But that's exactly what's happening.

"I'll take this to him," I offer, grabbing his coffee from the counter.

The humidity smacks me in the face when I step outside onto the sun baked patio. He's watching me, cradling my cup in his left hand.

"I think you picked up my drink on accident," I say when I reach his table.

"Did I?" He doesn't even look at the cup.

"This one is yours." I put his drink on the table, beside mine.

He twists the cup until he sees the name scribbled on the side. "Hmm. I guess so." He drinks from my cup again.

"They're making another for me," I say, suddenly unsure how to have a conversation.

He pulls his sunglasses off, laying them on the table, while his eyes focus on mine.

I swallow.

He's like something out of a magazine. A dusting of a beard is scattered across his jawline, like he forgot to shave this morning. His jaw, square and set firmly, gives him a rugged look.

He's wearing a black polo shirt, neatly tucked into a pair of jeans. The top button of the shirt is undone, and black ink swirls out from the opening.

"Harley." He says my name like we aren't meeting for the first time.

"Yes." I clear my throat. "That's my name."

He puts my cup down. "I think your drink is ready. Why don't you get your things and join me out here?"

I look through the window and see Jacob waving at me.

"I...uh..." I have a book. I usually spend an hour reading.

He reaches over the table, picks up my hand and squeezes.

"Get your things and bring them out here." He squeezes again.

My mouth dries as I stare deeper into his eyes. I can walk away, but at the same time I can't.

"All right." I nod and he lets me go.

I pick up my drink from Jacob, who's gone back to cleaning the steam machine, and then grab my bag and book from my corner table before going back outside. When I get to the table, Zack is on his feet, holding a chair out for me.

"Oh, you don't have to do that." I laugh a little.

"Hmm." He pinches his lips together once I'm sitting, and he's settled back in his seat. "What are you reading?" He picks up the novel resting on top of my bag and looks at the cover. "Little Women?" He quirks an eyebrow.

My face heats and I pluck it from his grasp.

"Yes." I shove it into my bag and move it to the third chair at the table.

"You've never read it before?"

"Oh, no I have. I read it every year." I snap my mouth shut.

"Hmm." He takes a sip of his coffee. "You like it that much?"

Not really, but it was the book we last read together.

"It's a good book." I decide to stay neutral.

"But do you enjoy it?" he presses, leaning toward me

enough that his shirt opens a bit more and even more of his tattoo is exposed.

"Oh. Well." I take a sip of my drink. "I guess."

"You guess?"

"Hey, Harley." Josephine and Sara, two girls I went to high school with, walk up to us.

"I thought it was you," Josephine says. She's wearing a pair of sunglasses with mirrored lenses, so all I see is myself staring up at her. Her lips, painted with thick red lipstick, curl upward.

"Hi." I grip my cup tighter.

"You're on summer break then?" Sara asks, sliding her gaze toward Zack.

"Yes."

Zack's foot touches mine beneath the table. Such a small gesture, but it helps settle my nerves.

"How's your mom?" Josephine asks with a sneer in her voice. She folds her arms over her chest.

"She's doing fine." I pick up my cup, take a sip like her presence isn't bothering me. Like I don't know what she's thinking. How she's judging me.

It's the same since it happened.

The same look. The same questioning attitude.

"Really? It's a hard time of year, isn't it?" Josephine prods.

"Yes. It is." The cardboard cup bends beneath my fingers, and I let go before I pop the cover off and make a mess.

Sara's eyes go to my hand then back to Zack. "Hi. I'm Sara." She extends her hand over the table toward him. "I haven't seen you around before."

Zack looks at her hand as though it drips with poison, and moves his hand to cover mine, squeezing a little. And just like with his foot, it settles my nerves. My stomach doesn't twist so hard beneath Josephine's glare.

Sara frowns and drops her hand.

"I'm new to town." Zack leans back, moving his arm to drape over my shoulders.

"And you're sitting with Harley?" Josephine pulls her sunglasses down her nose just enough to expose her brown eyes. They pierce me with her disdain, but Zack runs the tip of his thumb over my neck and I'm able to keep from hiding.

"I am." Zack looks to Sara. "Did you want something? We were in the middle of a conversation." His tone lowers, like he's chastising toddlers.

Josephine shoves her glasses back up her nose.

"I know this time of year is really hard on your mom. I hope you're doing the right thing and helping her through it." She nudges Sara.

"Enjoy your summer." Sara gives me a look filled with pity. I'm not sure how she deals with Josephine. I would have thought she'd be finished with putting up with the mean girl bullshit after we graduated, but maybe Josephine has worn her down too much for her to fight back.

"I will. Thanks. You too."

"See ya, *shadow*." Josephine turns hard on her high heeled sandals and pulls Sara along with her down the street.

Josephine's mother owns the boutique on the corner. They've been working there since high school. Not much changes in this town.

"Who was that?" Zack asks.

"Just some girls from school." I sigh, dropping my gaze to my coffee.

He moves his hand from around me to cup my chin, pulling my focus to him.

"Never lie to me, Harley." His words are slow, deliberate. "No matter what, never lie to me."

I swallow around the ball of nerves that's moved up to my throat now that we're alone again. Everything about him is intense, and it sets my insides on fire. But when he touches me, it all just sizzles away, and I'm at ease again.

"I'm not lying." I promise. "I did go to high school with them."

He searches my features.

"But there's more." Little wrinkles appear around his eyes as he narrows them.

"I don't even know you." I try to pull away, but he tightens his grasp on my chin, holding me steady. "You're being very bold."

"You will. I promise. But first, tell me, why did that girl make you feel so on edge? What did she mean by calling you shadow?"

My stomach knots up again.

"It's a horrible nickname. That's all." I wrap my hand around his wrist. "Really, they're just girls I went to high school with. Josephine's a bitch, always has been."

He moves his gaze to my hand.

"I think there's more here, but I understand you need time." He lets go of my chin and leans back into his chair. His knee presses against mine, though.

"You're new here you said, but I saw you the other day. And yesterday." I try for a lighthearted giggle. "You weren't following me, were you?"

His lips quirk up to the right. Keeping his gaze locked on mine, he brings his coffee cup to his lips and takes a long sip.

I look away from him, at the cars driving by on the street. I shouldn't have gone out today. I should be staying out of the public eye until this week is over. This week is always the worst one of the year. It's better when I'm not around, reminding everyone.

Townsend County spans over five hundred miles, most of them farmland. Hazel Corners is the main town in the county. Half the population of the county lives within these twenty square miles. Running into people from my past is inevitable.

An alarm rings, and he pulls out his phone, glancing at it before swiping away the notification.

I'm saved.

"I have a meeting I need to get to." He puts his phone away. "I'll ask an easy question. Why is this time of year hard on your mother?"

There's something so comfortable about his hard tone. It takes away my choice of whether or not to give in. I'm going to do what he says, because of him, because he's not giving me room to run away.

"It's because of something that happened a long time ago." I scoot back in my chair, ready to get up. He's leaving now, so I can go back inside where it's air conditioned, and I can read my book.

"What happened, Harley?" He digs into his wallet and pulls out a business card.

"You're going to be late for your meeting," I say.

He puts his hand on top of mine, drawing my attention to him again.

"Tell me."

I swallow.

"My sister was killed." The words flow out on a long breath. After eleven years, I would think it would be easier to say the words. But it still feels like someone else is talking when I say them.

His expression doesn't move. Did he already know? Most people are a little shocked when I say it out loud.

"We were kidnapped, and he killed her. Not me." I pause. "We were twins. She was popular, pretty, had a lot of friends. They called me her shadow - that's where the nickname came from."

"Josephine had a lot of attitude for it to be just a bad nickname from school," he pushes.

"She blames me. A lot of them blame me. The shadow survived." I try to laugh it off, but I only end up huffing.

"They blame you because between you and your sister, you weren't chosen?"

"No. Because I was."

FOUR

"Where's Mom?" My sister's soft voice cracks through the darkness.

"They took her a while ago," I answer, scooting as close to her as the thick metal chains bound to my ankles will allow.

The floor we sit on is dirty, and covered with a thick grime. It stinks of oil and gasoline in here, but there isn't enough light for me to make out more than a few feet around us.

And so far, all I've seen is the cement wall we're chained to, and the cement flooring.

"Are you all right?" I ask. My fingertips brush across hers.

Her chains clink against the floor as she shifts, trying to get closer to me.

"My side hurts, but yeah. I'm okay. Why are we here?"

"I don't know."

"I'm tired."

"I know." I get just close enough to squeeze her fingers. "I can't tell how long we've been here or what time it is. But maybe you should get some sleep." Maybe we both should.

Who knows what the monster has in store for us next?

When I work my jaw, it's still sore. Getting backhanded across the face hurts a hell of a lot more than it looks like in the movies.

"Why are they doing this to us?" Her voice is soft, like she's almost asleep. "Char–"

The door creaks open, drowning out her faint voice. Metal screeches as it moves, and light pours in from the opening. A figure stands in the light, making their features hard to make out.

"Good. You're both up." His voice crawls over me, thick like the grime covering the floor beneath us.

He drags his feet as he makes his way toward us. The heel of his shoe scrapes the floor with each step.

"Where's our mom?" I ask, fighting the tremor in my voice.

"Don't worry about her. She's safe enough." The closer he gets, the more my eyes are able to focus. "At least for now."

"What do you want with us?" my sister asks, scooting back against the wall and pulling her knees up to her chin. I can't reach her now, she's too far away.

The man squats between us, running his tongue over his top teeth. The stench of cigarette smoke rolls off him in thick waves. It's stifling how bad he smells.

"I haven't had a pair of sisters in a long time." He smacks his lips together, like he's been starved, and a full feast has been put in front of him. "It's going to be fun, the three of us playing together."

"Please. What do you want?" I draw his attention when his eyes linger on my sister for too long. She's already so tired and hurting from the last time he took her from the room. She won't tell me what he did, only that she's hurting. But before he slammed the door last time, the light caught her legs, and I noticed the blood on her thigh.

She can't go with him again.

"Fun. We're just having fun." He leans toward me. "I know you're sisters and all, but your tits aren't as big. It's like she got all the pretty and you got the scraps of what was left." He reaches his hand out to me, trying to cup my chin, but I slap his hand away.

Idiot move.

Stars burst in my vision, as sharp pain radiates from my jaw up to my ear. Another smack comes from the other direction. Loud ringing bursts in my ears.

"Mom...you'd be....or your sister..." I can't make out what he's yelling at me. The noise is too loud.

"I'm sorry!" I yell when he moves to the chains at my sister's ankles. "No! Take me! Take me!" My knees scrape against the rough concrete as I scramble toward him, pulling on his leg, hoping to get him away from her.

He shakes me off like I'm some annoying dog.

"Leave her alone!" I scream until my throat stretches around the words, but he's already got her unchained and yanked up to her feet. "Don't hurt her!" My voice cracks mid yell.

"Please," she whimpers.

"C'mon sweetheart, it's fine." He pulls her by her elbow. Her bare feet pad across the floor as he half drags her off toward the door. "We're just gonna have some fun. I ain't gonna hurt you, unless you make me."

"Stop!" The chains cut into my ankles as I lunge forward. "Please. Take me!"

He stops at the door, turns back to me.

"You're next, don't worry." And then he hurls my sister into the hallway and slams the door again, thrusting me back into darkness.

Only this time, I'm all alone.

Just me and the monsters.

FIVE

Zack

If it wasn't for this asshole, I would have been able to stay with Harley longer.

But I've never strayed from a plan before, and today will be no different. I'm just going to have to make Mr. Carpenter pay a little more for fucking up my day.

I knew Harley was special. I could sense it from the moment our eyes met in that cafe, two days ago. And then, when I saw her with her mother at that grocery store, it only cemented the idea that something deep inside of her was yearning to be released.

There's a great pain inside her.

And I'm going to help her get it out.

But first, this fucker.

I pull my car around to the back of the barn. It's already getting dark, but I keep my lights off.

No need to warn him I'm here just yet.

After I get the tools and things I need, I leave the car parked and make my way to the barn. The door is still bolted shut from the outside, so I'm confident he's still tucked inside, safe and sound.

Just like he designed.

And he is.

There he is, in all his fucking asshole glory.

Little mumblings echo from the chamber he's tucked inside of, so I kick the lid away and peer down at him.

Naked, he sits with his knees pulled to his chin. It's the only position he can be in, unless he wants to remain standing.

And two days of standing upright would have been hell.

I would have preferred it for him. But I have a code to stick to, and that's what I've done here.

He gets what he gave.

Slowly, he turns his face up to me, wincing at the brightness of the flashlight I have beaming in his eyes.

"Please," he whimpers, shivering from the cold. It's hot outside, but sitting with no clothes on in an underground cell with only a three-foot circumference has left him chilled. Maybe it's the concrete walls.

I move the light from his face to the bucket next to him. He's utilized it a few times in the last two days.

"Please, what, Dustin?" I ask.

"Please. Just let me go."

I roll my eyes.

Pathetic.

"I'm disappointed. It's like you haven't been paying attention at all." I grab the rope ladder and drop it down the well. "Come on up and bring your toilet with you." I keep the light shining on the hole as I step back.

Slowly, he makes his way up. The metal bucket clanks against the cement wall as he makes his ascent. I couldn't have cared less if he shit himself while he was down there, but he'd let Jessica have it when he kept her locked up down there.

Once he scrambles to the floor of the barn, I turn on the set of painter's lights, illuminating the area.

"Leave the bucket there. And go to the center." I point to the table in the middle of the lights.

He looks over at the setup—he should be familiar with it—and blanches. For a second, I think he's going to puke, but he composes himself.

"Look. I'm sorry. Please." He bends over, pressing his hands into his knees and sucking air. His hair is matted to his head, filthy and sweating from his captivity. "I'll confess. Please, just call the police."

I stare at him. I can't help it. There are levels of stupidity, and this man has reached every single one of them.

"Did you call the police when you had Jessica here?" I stalk toward him until he hurries his step to the table. He stops short of climbing on.

Panicked eyes meet mine.

"Oh god no." He sobs, breaking down just like a little baby. I shouldn't blame him. He's just realized, finally, what's about to happen to him. It's a lot to take in, but really, this is on him. He should have known.

"Now, Dustin, we've repeated every step, haven't we? Did you really think we wouldn't play out the last bit?" I drop a manila folder on the surgical table, throwing it open and splaying out the photographs inside.

I jam my finger at the police report.

"Hogtied and left in trunk of a car. See, there's the bruising from the tire iron you had her lying on." I grab his head, forcing him to face the photograph of the ugly bruise on the poor girl's side.

He sobs again, tries to pull away, but he's been weakened by his ride in the trunk, and then two more days in the pit. He's not going anywhere.

"Then an estimated forty-eight to seventy-two hours underground." I point to the pictures of her broken fingernails.

Two of them had come clean off. Traces of cement and

dirt were found beneath what was left. I smack the back of his head, sending his forehead into the table.

"Look at the photos. Look at the cuts, the scrapes, look at the finger bruises you left on her thighs!" I punch him in the gut, making him fall to the ground with a grunt.

"I'm sorry. So sorry," he sobs, rolling to his side and curling his knees up to his chin.

"I know you are." I nod. "But it's not enough. Nothing I do to you will be enough." I grab hold of his hair, yanking him back to his feet. He's a short man. Although he's got an athletic build, there's not much to him.

"An eye for an eye, Dustin." I pull my knife from where I keep her holstered at my back. "Now, get on the table and lie on your fucking back."

The dirt on his face runs off with his tears. His eyelashes are wet. Drool slips from his mouth, and snot runs from his nose.

He's fucking repulsive. But it changes nothing.

He manages to get up on the table and lies back, his hands at his sides, and his eyes screwed shut. If he thinks the end is coming, he's wrong. There's still one more thing to do before I end him.

Before I drag my knife from his throat to his pelvis, just like he did to poor Jessica. A complete hack job, and it won't be any prettier when I do it.

Seventeen years old. He stole her, he hurt her, he destroyed her, and then he killed her.

Death is too easy for him, but it's all I can offer.

I flick his flaccid cock with the tip of my knife.

"Get to it."

His eyes fly open. "W-what?" Confusion fills those beady little eyes of his.

"This is where we'll deviate just a little," I explain to him, grabbing the picture of Jessica and using the tip of my knife to point at the bruising on her thighs. "You hurt her using that little cock of yours, yes?"

He swallows.

"I'll take that as a confession. I'm not gonna touch your little prick. You'll do it. Go on, get yourself off." I grab his hand and shove it on his groin. "Do it."

"Why? You'll just kill me anyway." Ah, some sense has finally made its way back to his brain.

"That's right. I am going to kill you, just like you killed that girl. But I'm happy to deviate a little more and start removing body parts before that happens."

All color drains from his face.

"A toe. A finger. Another toe. Some of your thigh. A little bit of fat from your ass. I mean, there's a lot I can remove before I get to anything vital." I tap my knife to my cheek. "If I were you, I'd start thinking about something to get that dick hard."

He closes his eyes, swallows again.

It takes a few minutes, but finally his cock stiffens. Right along with every muscle in my body. I know what he's thinking about to get himself hard. I want to pummel his face in for it, but I have to keep steady.

"Go on." I nudge his thigh with the knife.

He's slow at first. But in seconds he's going at it like a pubescent high schooler who just learned how good his own hand feels.

Just when I think the fucker can't be any more repulsive, he starts fucking moaning.

Moaning!

I grip the handle of my knife. This can't be finished soon enough.

His eyes are closed while he's licking his lips.

Jessica didn't get any reprieve. She saw no pleasure during the three days she was his captive. She was beaten and bruised. He'd taken the very essence of her.

He can't possibly think I'm letting him bust his nut before this is over.

But he does. The monster actually thinks he's going to orgasm.

He's pumping harder, faster, and his lips are trembling.

I poise the knife.

"All right, Dustin. Open up, sweet boy."

Just as his eyes open, I strike, plunging the knife right into his throat.

SIX

Harley

A thick cloud of cotton candy vape floats across the bar and into my face. I follow the cloud to a college kid standing in the crowd, with an empty beer glass.

"Hey!" I lean over the bar and yell. I can barely hear myself over the music thumping in the background. Carl brought in a DJ for the weekends. It worked in attracting more customers, but it's also made it hell to hear anyone.

"Hey!" I wave my hand toward the kid as he brings the vape back to his mouth. "You can't do that in here. You gotta go outside!" I jerk my thumb toward the front door.

He frowns.

"It's not smoke," he argues, yelling over the two people standing in front of him waiting for their turn to be served.

"I don't care. You can't do it here. Outside," I yell back, then lean in to hear the girl who's ordering her third rum and Coke of the night. I snag her cash and get the drink for her.

"You got those guys over there?" Carl, the owner and second bartender for the night gestures to the line in front of me.

"Yeah, I'm good." I place the glass on a cocktail napkin and push it toward the girl. "Here you go."

She smiles as she takes it, then turns into the crowd and is swallowed by it.

I take the next orders, quickly making my way through the kids waiting for their drinks. Checking my watch, I sigh with some relief. Only an hour left of my shift.

The time sails by when it's busy like this, and every Friday night is crazy. I love my teaching job, but I've only been on the payroll for three years. Not exactly high up on the pay scale. Working here over the summer helps pack away cash.

"What can I get you?" I ask, feeling someone step up while I'm cleaning some glasses.

"Whiskey." A deep voice rolls over the bar, wrapping around me. A warm tingle runs through me.

When I look up, I confirm what my body already knew.

"Zack." I smile before I can help myself. The pull this man has on me is unreal. It's like his energy sucks me into him the moment he gets near me.

"Hey." He grins.

"Sorry. Whiskey, you said?" I blink a few times after I realize I'm staring at him.

He just gives a little nod. I get his drink for him and put it on the bar.

"Are you here with anyone?" I ask, looking for a group of friends maybe, or a girl. What if he's with a girl?

The stab of jealousy surprises me.

"No." He lays a fifty down on the bar and slides it to me. "Keep the change."

"That's too much. I can't." I pick up the bill.

"You can. And you will." He arches that eyebrow again.

I keep quiet while I tap the transaction into the iPad.

"What brings you here then?" I look behind him to be sure there's no one waiting on a drink. It's starting to slow down now that it's almost closing. The college kids have filed out to find a bar that's open past two, and the regulars are starting to pour themselves into cabs to roll home to sleep it off.

"You." He takes a small sip of the whiskey.

"How'd you know I work here?" I tilt my head. "Are you following me again?"

He laughs.

"I'm really good at getting information I want," he says.

"And you wanted to know where I work?"

"I want to know more than that, but I figured I'd do the normal thing and let you tell me." He winks and takes another sip.

The last time a man winked at me, I was serving him a cup of coffee at the professors' luncheon my senior year. He thanked me with a pinch on my ass and a wink.

No one noticed.

He winked a second time when I walked past his table with a tray of cheesecake slices and asked me for more coffee.

When I returned with a freshly brewed pot of coffee, the woman sitting next to him asked for a cup as well. I shook my head at her and moved his cup to the edge of the table so I could get a good pour. And then, I poured the pot of piping hot coffee into his lap.

He screamed and bolted up from his chair, knocking it and me out of the way. I only got to spill half the coffee on him, but he still went home with fresh burns to his thighs.

I lost my job.

It was worth it.

But when I look at Zack, and he winks, it's not the same. There's no crudeness here. Just confidence and charm.

"Hey! I know you!" a man slurs as he slides up next to Zack, trying to shove him out of the way so he can get in front of me.

But Zack doesn't move, he's like a brick wall.

The drunk man has no idea what's happening, so he just stays pressed up against Zack.

"Can I get you something? A cup of coffee maybe?" I ask. He's clearly drunk.

He shakes his head while wagging his finger at me.

"No. No. I know you. You're that girl." He snaps his fingers, looking from me to Zack. "You know, the girl. She was on the news last night."

My stomach twists. I don't know why I thought this year would be any different. There's always some journalist who wants to dredge up the past. They always say it's in the name of justice. Bringing more eyes to the case might help solve it.

Truth is, they just want the ratings. And our story brings the ratings.

"Here. On the house." I pour a cup of lukewarm coffee and slide it across the bar at him. The music's lower now. There's almost no one on the dance floor anymore and the DJ is getting ready to pack up.

"You're...fuck, what's your name?" His bushy eyebrows knit together and his mouth puckers as he tries to place me.

"Why don't you take your coffee and find a place to sober up?" Zack brings the cup closer to the drunkard, but it only pisses him off more.

His brows knit together and his bloodshot, watery eyes narrow.

"Quinn!" He snaps his fingers again, then his mouth splits into a grin, exposing a missing tooth.

A chill runs up my back. "No. That was my sister. Please, go drink your coffee."

"Shit. Sorry." He frowns. "You're the other one. The one that didn't get killed. Man, I'm sorry about that. What happened? That was horrible." He's rambling now. "But all the money, that had to be good right?" He laughs a little.

Zack reaches behind the guy, and grabs him by the back of his shirt collar.

"She doesn't want to talk to you. Last chance to walk away." Zack's eyes narrow, his entire presence is like a storm cloud barreling down on us. The chill turns warm as it runs through my body.

This man is dangerous.

I can see in his eyes; he has no problem bringing this drunk asshole pain.

"I was just asking." The drunk shakes his head. "I mean, your sister gets blown away right in front of you and it could have been you, wow. Right? I mean, if you had been the one chosen to die instead of live? Yeah. Wow. Really fucks with your brain." He's still rambling when Zack yanks him from the stool and drops him to the floor.

"I think that's enough tonight." Zack doesn't give him a chance to get up, he just stalks toward the exit, dragging the drunk guy along with him like a pet rock on a leash.

"What's going on?" Carl runs up to me.

"The guy was causing a problem. Don't worry, he's leaving," I say, my face heats.

"Who's the guy dragging him?"

"That's Zack," I say with a small tug on my lips.

"Zack, huh?" Carl looks at me and shakes his head. "Just make sure there's nothing to clean up. Why don't you clock out? Me and Jason can close up tonight."

"You sure?"

He glances at Zack, who's walking back inside from the front door, without the drunk, and he nods. "Yeah. I think you have better things to do tonight anyway." Carl takes the cup of untouched coffee. "Besides, it's about time you had something other than a book to keep you company at night."

He laughs at his own cleverness and walks away.

"He's gone." Zack says, planting his hands on the bar. "He won't be back, either."

"You didn't hurt him, did you?" I can't pretend that I'm not a little excited at the idea that maybe he did.

"He'll live." There's a splotch of blood on his knuckles. He follows my gaze to it. "Not mine."

"Good." I take his hand and wipe the blood away with my towel. "Thanks. You didn't have to do that though."

"He was bothering you."

"It's this time of year," I explain. "The news will run a few stories about what happened. I'll get a few people who recognize me, and then in a few weeks, it will all blow over."

"Doesn't give him the right to poke a wound."

"Guess not."

"You off soon?"

"I'm off now."

"Good." He retracts his hand. "Get your stuff. I'll take you home."

"Maybe I have my car." I'm flirting, and it's the most normal thing I've done in ages.

"You don't have a car, Harley Turner." He winks again.

"How do you know that?"

"I told you; I make it my business to know what I want to know. Now, let's go."

It takes me no time at all to grab my purse and punch out for the night. Then Zack leads me to his car, parked in a lot on the next street over.

I stop as he opens the passenger door for me. A single streetlamp shines down on the empty lot, casting him in a shadow as he holds the door open for me.

"I'm not sure." I hold my purse in front of me, as though it could protect me from him. I don't think anything would protect against this man when he wants something.

"Not sure about what?" he asks, not at all pissed about my hesitation. He's patient. He'll wait until I'm ready.

It's weird how much I can sense about him.

"How do I know you won't hurt me? That you're not some serial killer?" Considering my past, I should have some radar for this.

He steps up to me until his toes press against my sneakers.

The heavy scent of leather and spice fills the space between us as he slips both hands into my hair, pulling my head back.

"I will never hurt you, Harley. I promise, and I never break my promises." He seals his vow with a kiss, a soft kiss that turns hard and possessive within a breath.

And I'm lost to it. Lost to him.

A storm could burst right on top of us, but all I would feel, would know, is his touch and him.

"All right," I say breathlessly when he breaks contact and pulls back just enough for me to see his eyes. "Do you need directions to my apartment?"

He flashes a lopsided grin.

"What do you think?" And then he winks again.

Playful and sexy.

"No. You don't."

SEVEN

Zack

"Which one?" I ask as we stand in front a pair of doors.

Harley freezes.

"Which one is it?" I ask again, laying a hand on her shoulder. She jumps.

"What?" She twists toward me. "What did you say?"

"Which apartment?" I gesture to the stairs.

"Oh." She breathes a sigh of relief, like she's just realized she's here at home and not somewhere else. Wherever she thought she was for those few seconds, it terrified her.

"This one." She starts up the stairs to the left.

"That guy at the bar." I'm opening the box I'm sure she wants to weld shut, but doing that will only make things harder later. She's harboring pain, and I can't have that.

It doesn't belong to her anymore.

"Yeah?" Harley slides her key into the deadbolt lock on her apartment door. She lives above a dry cleaner, a mile away from the bar. The shop below is closed, but the aroma of chemical steam clings to the air.

"Does that happen a lot?" I ask, shutting the door behind me once we're inside.

The air is cool inside the apartment, and the stench from outside hasn't creeped in. It smells of vanilla and cinnamon. Probably from the candles on the coffee table.

The apartment is small; there's a kitchen, with a two-person table, that leads directly into the living space where she has an oversized armchair and a loveseat facing the television. Three bookcases line the exterior wall.

Simple, but I can still feel her here.

She drops her purse and keys on the kitchen table before turning to me.

"Around now, yes." She goes to the fridge, bending over to look inside. The light hits her face, shining on a raised scar. It's thin, and runs from her cheekbone to her ear.

"Because of the news?" I lean my hip against the counter.

She grabs a bottle of water for herself and offers one to me. I take it.

"Yes." She opens her bottle, takes a sip. "They think they're helping, but they're not." She hesitates, then screws the cap back on.

"Help how?" I've never seen anything helpful about the media.

"I told you my sister was murdered. They never caught the guy." She walks to the love seat and sinks down, tucking her feet beneath her. The V-neck T-shirt she's wearing pulls tight around her chest when she leans back and my gaze dips to the swell of her breasts.

"He said you witnessed it." I know everything that happened, but I want her to tell it.

"I did." She nods, then leans to the coffee table and puts the bottle of water down. "It's not a fun story, Zack."

I shake my head. "No. I wouldn't think so. But that's the second time someone's brought it up this week."

"Next Friday is the anniversary." She sighs and folds her arms over her stomach.

I take the seat next to her, sitting sideways so I can face her.

"Tell me," I order her, laying my hands on her knees.

She looks away for a second, and when she looks back her jaw is firm.

"You didn't read about it already? I mean a quick Google search would tell you everything."

It wouldn't tell me anything about her experience though, only the webs journalists spin to get clicks. It's not information about what happened that I want, it's her I want to know. "I want you to tell me." There is so much to learn about her, and I crave all the knowledge on the subject I can get.

Her gaze wanders over my face, searching for something. I won't react. I only want to take in her memories.

"I can't." She shakes her head a little. "Not because I don't want to, because I really can't. Everything I remember is all jumbled up in my head." She taps her temple. "Parts of it are missing, and other parts I'm not sure are right."

"It was a traumatic thing, it's reasonable that your brain would try to hide the memory from you." In my experience, the memory will find a way out, though.

Her eyes narrow on me. Suspicion fills her gaze.

"You're not one of those journalists, are you?" She jumps from the love seat, like being near me might hurt her.

"Of course not." I'm not even offended she asks. Girl like her, with what happened to her, needs to be sure.

"Then why do you keep asking about this? You're just trying to get a story, like all of them. You want to know what it felt like, to sit there with a gun to my head, to my sister's head, while my mom was forced to make a choice. You want to know." Her chest heaves, and she steps back again, bumping into the television.

"Harley, I swear, I'm no journalist." I slide my legs off the couch, press my elbows into my knees. I won't touch her, not yet, but if she creeps too close the cliff, I may have to drag her back.

"You just happened to show up this week?" She laughs with no joy. I wonder when she last held on to happiness for more than a fleeting moment.

"I did." I nod. "I had work that brought me to town, but then I saw you." I keep my tone even. I didn't just see her, I felt her. She sank into my skin. I'm hungry for more.

"Maybe this was a mistake." She walks to the door, flips the lock, and yanks it open. "You should go."

I'm doing no such thing.

I lean back, cross my foot over my knee.

"Close the door, Harley," I instruct, still keeping my voice level. She's unsure of herself right now, but it's not because of me. It's her mind. She's trying to recall things, but they're not there, not in the right order. Or they're lying to her.

Having your mind lie to you is beyond reason.

"You already know," she whispers. "And you don't want to leave?"

"Why would I want to leave? I'm exactly where I want to be. I'm never where I don't want to be." I point a finger at her. "And you don't have to be anymore, either."

Moments tick by as her eyes bore into me. She's thinking, and I won't interrupt the process.

It's a full minute before she slowly shuts the door and turns the bolt.

"You don't understand how messed up I am, Zack," she says, coming back to me on the love seat and sinking back into her space.

"Everyone's messed up to a degree." I reach out to her, tuck her hair behind her ear. "Me included." If she only knew how true that statement is.

"No." She shakes her head. "I know what happened, at least what the record says happened. Mom tried to keep me all the news stories from me, but it's been eleven years. Of course I've heard them, seen them. But what they say happened, and what I remember, are so different. And then there're the chunks completely missing. Sometimes I think I'm going to go crazy if I don't find out the truth."

"The truth about who did it?" I scoot closer to her, comfortable now that she won't bolt on me.

She nods. "The news runs the story every year because they say it will help find the guy, but it won't. No one really wants to find him. My mom doesn't even push for it. She only–" She cuts off her words, and sighs. "She has her own troubles with all of this," she says after a moment.

"Well, she lost a child. I can't imagine the sort of pain that causes." The sort it should cause, I understand. I've seen too much in the last fifteen years to think that every parent reacts the same way to losing a child. I don't even count on every parent having grief over it anymore.

That's the trouble with my career choice. Gave me too much information on the reality of the world. It's hard to look through any other lens besides the one this sick and twisted place has given me.

But there's a light inside Harley, and maybe she can bring me closer to it.

"It's not that. I mean it is, but it's more. She has so much guilt."

I nod. The files didn't go into much detail about her mother, other than she was present as well. I couldn't find any interview notes with her. It will take a little more digging.

My reach can only go so far before flags are thrown.

I have to be careful. "I'm sure. She couldn't save your sister."

She brings her eyes in line with mine.

"No, Zack. It's not that." She swallows. "He gave her a choice." She pauses again, taking a breath. "And she chose me."

EIGHT

Soft whimpers from beside me make my chest ache. The fear, the pain, rises in my chest along with hers, but there's nothing I can do. Nothing any of us can do.

There's been a fog lingering in my mind since I woke up a little while ago. There must have been something in the water he finally let us have.

My head throbs.

Metal creaks and the door opens again. A bright light hit my face and the door slams shut. Booted footsteps echo. I turn away from the sound, looking toward my mom. Bound and silenced by a gag, she stares down the man walking towards us. Her cheeks shimmer with tears when the flashlight beam hits her.

"Good. Everyone's awake." A second set of footsteps draw my attention. Another man steps out from behind the first. Two men. The first one I've seen before; he's been here a lot. But my mind is heavy, and a lot of drugs have been pumped into my arm. I couldn't be certain if the second guy was actually there at all, much less if he was the same guy.

"This here is my friend." He slaps the second guy on the shoulder. His friend looks us over, licking his lips like a dog ready to devour his dinner.

I stare at him, forcing myself not to give in to the fear rattling my ribs. I need to play nice for now.

"You've got your pick," he says, standing in front of my mom. "Dear ole Mommy here." He yanks her gag out, letting the rag hang around her neck.

"Stop this! You have to stop!" she yells, but he raises his hand, sending the back of it across her face.

"I already told you to keep quiet. Keep it up, and I'll take out your tongue." He jabs a finger at her.

She sniffles and hangs her head while nodding.

"Then there're these two." He shuffles over to my sister, cupping her chin and pushing it back. "They're sisters. This one has prettier eyes, I think." He shoves her bangs away from her face. The light from his flashlight exposes the dirt on her cheeks.

She keeps quiet when he pulls the rag from her mouth. Opening and closing her jaw, she works the stiffness out before turning to look at me. Tears shimmer in her eyes.

"This one though." He steps over to me, shining the light right in my eyes. I wince at the sudden pain and turn away. "This one has a prettier mouth." He jerks my gag out, letting it dangle around my neck before sticking his thumb into my mouth and yanking my jaw open.

I fight, but he bound my hands behind my back after I tried to gouge out his eyes the last time he came in. It's useless, this fighting. And every time I do, he threatens my sister, my mother. I'm going to get them killed if I keep it up.

"Leave them alone! Please. This isn't supposed to be happening. This isn't supposed to be happening," Mom cries, shaking her head, like she wants to wake herself from a bad dream.

"Don't hurt her," I say when his jaw tightens again.

"Please," I beg. Bruises already cover Mom's cheek from his slap.

"She's a little tougher this one." He pats my face and steps closer to me, straddling me until I can feel his erection pressed against my arm. "But she's sweet once you get her settled down."

I swallow the vomit rolling up my throat and turn away, looking to my sister.

"Have a look," he tells his friend, then steps away.

A beam of light hits my face, then moves to my sister, then to Mom. I whine, trying to draw his attention away, but he moves to stand in front of my sister.

"How much she been used? I don't want your sloppy leftovers." He picks up a lock of her blonde hair and rubs it between his tobacco-stained fingers.

"By me? Only twice. She's tight though, you won't even notice," the first man says.

"Don't touch her!" I yell when he moves to cup her cheek. I jerk my body, trying to get my hands loose.

A flash of light hits me—stars dancing in my vision just before the sharp pain ricochets through my head. When will I learn?

He leans in, the stale stench of cigarettes and whiskey hit my face.

"See, I told you. This one has a lot of fight in her." He jams his finger beneath my chin and shoves my head back. "But it's a hell of a lot of fun getting her to settle." He taps my cheek.

"Leave her be. Please. Leave them be," Mom whimpers beside me.

"Isn't that right?" The tip of a knife presses against my cheek. "You're a sweet thing once you've had a good beating, and a good fucking. Isn't that right?"

Every time I move, I feel the memory of his idea of settling me down.

"Please, just leave us alone," I say, as softly as I can to keep him from getting pissed again.

He presses the knife harder into my cheek. Blood slides down my cheek, dripping off my chin.

"That's not going to happen, sweetheart. I'm not done playing." He pulls the knife away, and wipes my blood onto what's left of my shirt. It's torn and tattered in so many places, it might as well not be on anymore.

"Well now she's fucking bleeding," the second man scoffs, shining his light on my face. "I don't want her blood all over me." He moves the beam to my sister. "I'll take this one. You're right about her eyes."

"Good call," the first man says and shoves a rag into my mouth, dragging the other rag over it to gag me. I scream into it anyway.

He moves to my mother and does the same. The rag soaks up her cries.

I lunge toward my sister, but without my hands, I can't get to my feet properly. I fall over in my scrambles. It's useless. I can't stop him.

The second man grabs the back of her hair, dragging her up to her feet once her chains have been undone.

She screams.

She cries.

She begs.

"Please! No! No! Please!" Her voice echoes against the walls of our hell.

I scream into my gag.

The door slams.

The light is all gone.

My mother whimpers.

NINE

Harley

A scream wakes me, hurtling me upright in bed.

"Harley?" Zack's here, he's pulling at my hands that are clawing at the bedding, trying to untangle myself.

It was me.

I'm screaming.

"Harley. It's all right." He gets the blankets out of my grasp and throws them off me, pulling me right into his lap as he leans back against the headboard of my bed.

Zack's here.

In my bed.

I blink, pushing the sleep and horror from my eyes so I can focus on his face.

His beautiful, stern, worried face.

"I'm so sorry." I whisper, covering my mouth with my fingertips. "It's been so long since that's happened."

He wipes my hair from my face. It's stuck in place by the thin layer of sweat.

"It's all right. You were having a nightmare. It happens."

He tucks the last bit of hair behind my ear and cups my cheek, drawing my face toward his. "It's all right. You're okay."

I take a shaky breath and nod.

"I'm okay." I agree. I'm here. I survived.

The guilt crushes me.

"Harley. Look at me." His voice hardens. His grip on my cheek tightens. "Look at me."

I blink. Aren't I? No. I'm staring at the headboard over his head. Still lost in the fog of my miserable past. I'll never outrun it. It drowns me even when I sleep.

I move my eyes to his and blink.

"I'm sorry," I say again.

He frames my face with both hands, holding me firmly.

"You have nothing to be sorry for." His chin lowers. "It's no wonder, after everything you told me tonight. Of course you'd have a nightmare." He pulls me closer, tucking my head beneath his chin.

I melt right into him.

The nightmare clears away, and the reality of the evening focuses better now.

After we'd finished talking, it was nearly three in the morning. I'd asked if he wanted to just sleep here instead of going back to his motel.

"I'm glad you stayed," I say, after silent moments pass. "Sometimes the nightmares turn into panic attacks once I'm awake."

He lightly pets my cheek.

"Are you having one now?"

I shake my head, bumping into his chin.

"No." I sigh and wrap my arms around him. "I'm all right. It's gone now."

"What's gone?"

"The memory." I take a deep breath. "Or the nightmare. I'm not sure anymore. It gets all muddled."

He runs a hand up and down my arm.

"Probably why they never got close to finding the guy. I can't be relied on. When my memories don't line up with Mom's, it makes it harder."

His eyebrows knit together.

"Your memory isn't your fault. The police have plenty of resources at their disposal. They shouldn't have had to rely on your recollection." He tilts his head.

"Maybe, but Special Agent Laurens never had much hope about finding him. They never closed the case, but the last time I spoke with her, she gave me her card and said to call her if I had anything for her. I got the impression they weren't working it anymore."

"Special Agent? She's FBI?"

"Yeah. It's a kidnapping case, so the FBI took it."

"When's the last time you talked to her?"

I think for a beat. "Two years ago? Maybe longer. But I think Mom calls her every year, around now, to see if they've made any progress."

"You and your mom don't talk much about your sister, do you?"

"It's better when we don't. The guilt...it hurts us both so much. We don't even celebrate my birthday anymore. Quinn was my twin."

He goes to ask another question, but pauses. A smile creeps across his lips.

"Harley, your twin sister's name is Quinn? You two were Harley Quinn?" He laughs. It's been so long since I heard such a beautiful sound, and while talking about my sister.

The weight of the nightmare eases.

I can't help but laugh a little too.

"My dad was a huge fan of comic books." I shrug. "Mom let him name us since we weren't boys." I roll my eyes, but it's sarcastic. Dad never once treated us anything other than his prized daughters. He wouldn't have traded us for anything.

"I bet the two of you did the name proud." He brushes his

fingertips along my cheek. "You should still celebrate your birthday," he says firmly.

"If the guy's ever caught. Maybe then. But now, it just feels wrong. I don't want to hurt Mom any more than she's been hurt." I frown and tap my temple. "I told you; I'm broken."

He pulls my hand down to my lap.

"You're not broken." He rests his hand on my knee and plays with the hem of my nightshirt. "I'm going to help you."

"Help me?" I laugh a little. "How?"

"We're going to find out who did this to you."

He sounds so confident in his statement. I'm not sure I want to think too hard about it. "The police, the FBI did try." Not too hard, I think. But I was so caught up in my own mess, I'm not sure I'm remembering that, or anything, right.

"They failed. You can't always depend on them." He runs his hand up my leg, just above my knee. "But you can always depend on me. Understand?" His tone hardens again.

"You've just met me, why do you want to help?"

He leans in. "Sometimes you meet someone who just clicks with you, you know? Like two pieces of a puzzle, they just fit. Do you know what I mean?"

"Yeah?"

"That's us, Harley. We're two pieces that fit together. And when it happens, you don't argue with it." His hand slides higher up my leg and I tense.

"Zack." I push against his hand, but he moves it higher, then starts to feel around the inside of my thigh.

Tears build, but I blink them away.

It's better he learns now.

This is who I am.

Broken.

"What is this?" He shoves my nightshirt up and sits up more so he can get a better look at the mess I've made.

Reaching over, he flicks on the side table lamp and all of the scars are exposed.

"Don't," I whisper as he lightly traces each jagged scar on both my thighs. The insides, the outsides, the tops, everywhere I could reach. Anywhere I could hide with a long pair of shorts or skirt.

"Did you do this?" He levels me with a hard stare and for a moment I think he's going to toss me off his lap and storm out. It wouldn't be the first time. Who wants to look at this mess, much less touch it?

"Harley. No lies, remember." He doesn't so much as blink. "Did you do this?"

I nod.

His eyes soften, and he returns his stare to my legs.

"You were trying to make the pain on the inside come out." He traces a long scar. It's raised, and uglier than the others. I'd cut too deep. I almost needed to get stitches for that one.

"I just wanted the pain to match." I cover his hand with mine, but he shakes it off.

"I'm not done looking." He shifts me so that he can see the other leg better, the outside of my thigh.

"It's ugly. I know."

His gaze snaps up to me.

"Nothing about you is ugly, Harley. And don't say it again." There's a warning there, and I'm not going to tempt it.

When he's finished his inspection, he moves me from his lap so I'm sitting next to him on the bed again.

He pushes my legs apart to kneel between them.

Capturing my face between his hands, he leans down, bringing his mouth just a breath from mine.

"From now on, you don't do this." He pushes my head back, lining up our gazes.

His stare is too intense; I have to look away. A bubble forms in my chest, and it's painful, it's pleasureful, I can't tell the difference. And the longer I stare into his beautiful eyes, the bigger the bubble gets.

"Harley," he snaps my name until I meet his eyes again. "You don't ever do this again, understood? If you need this, you tell me."

I blink.

"Tell me you understand."

"I understand," I say, because I do.

His mouth crashes down over mine. It's a deep kiss, hard and unyielding and I melt right into it.

I mewl when he bites down on my lip. He releases me a breath later, bringing his gaze to line with mine again.

"I'm the only one who gets to hurt you, Harley. Do you understand?"

I press my hands against his chest. "I understand, Zack."

"When it's too much, you tell me." He runs the back of his hand across my cheek. "I'll make it better. I'll make it the same for you."

"Yes, Zack." I nod and lean into him, pressing my lips against his. At first, I'm sure he's going to push me away. But he doesn't.

He wraps his hand around the back of my neck, and he pushes his body into me until my back is pressed against the mattress. His hand sinks into my hair, tugging it at its roots.

My body hums with the pain, and I wrap my arms around him, holding him to me, afraid he'll float away if I don't.

His free hand slides down my body until he gets to the hem of my nightshirt. Bunching it up in his hand, he pushes it up over my hips.

"These panties need to go," he mutters against my lips. "I want to feel you, Harley. All of you." He leans up on his forearm. A tingle is left on my scalp where he held my hair.

"Yes," I agree. I want that too. No. I need it.

"If you take them off, I'm going to fuck you." He says this so softly, I almost miss how threatening it sounds.

"Yes."

"You can say no." He palms my cheek. "You should probably say no, because once I have you. I'm never going to let you go."

"You say that like it should be bad, but it doesn't feel bad." I nibble on my lip.

"I don't ever want to make you feel bad."

"Only when I need you to?"

His lips kick up at the edges. "Only when you beg me to."

My core melts at the way he emphasizes his statement.

"You're basically a stranger."

He nods. "But it doesn't feel like that."

"No," I agree. "It doesn't. It feels like I've known you forever." How can that be when we've only met days ago? And yet, I've told him things I've never told anyone before.

And he's here in my bed. Cuddling me after a nightmare. Vowing to help me search out the truth.

He presses his body against mine and his erection pushes against my panties. I bite down on my bottom lip.

"Has any other man touched you here?" He reaches between us and cups my sex. My panties are already wet, soaked through from him being so close, so wonderfully sexy.

"Yes." I frown. "I'm twenty-five, Zack, of course I've had sex."

He arches an eyebrow. "When." Not a question, a demand.

"In college." Is he going to get up and leave now? I'm dirty.

He gives a hard nod. "And you've always said yes?"

"No. Not the first time." I lower my gaze.

"Hey, give me your eyes." His voice is soft, caressing. "Not your fault."

I nod. "I know."

"Good."

I smile a little. He doesn't think I'm dirty.

"Your panties are still on." He nudges me with a kiss to my chin, then my cheek, before taking my mouth again.

"Oh." I laugh when he goes back to staring at me. "Right." I hook my thumbs into the elastic of my panties and shove them down enough to get one leg out, then the other. Zack has to push up into a plank to allow me to move freely beneath him.

But as soon as I'm done, and the panties are on the floor, he quickly shoves out of his boxers.

Zack takes my hands and puts them over my head, capturing both my wrists beneath one of his hands.

"Is this all right?" he asks, leaning down to kiss my neck.

"Yes." I nod, bumping into his chin again. He grins at me.

"Open your legs for me, little bird. Open wide." He pulls my nightshirt up until my breasts are exposed. Leaning down, he plucks one nipple with his teeth.

I hiss because he's scraped the sensitive skin, and it burns.

"Hmm, I like that sound. Let's do it again." He moves to the opposite breast and does it again, this time biting down harder on the tip.

I suck in a breath and wiggle beneath him. The sting courses straight through my body to my very core.

The tip of his cock presses against my entrance.

"You're already so wet for me, so hot." He reaches between us and strokes his cock, rubbing the head through my folds until he's coated with my juices.

"Don't tease me, Zack," I chastise, arching upward at him.

He arches a brow. "Now I'm going to tease you even longer."

"No. Please." I shake my head. "I need you." I bite my lip. "I need you to touch me. Please."

"Since you asked so sweetly." He trails one finger up through my pussy lips, collecting my arousal. "Like that?" He brings his finger to his mouth and sucks the wetness off. "So sweet."

He lines his cock up with my entrance.

"I can be gentle if you want." His jaw is tight. I think it might hurt him if he has to hold back, and I know it will hurt me.

"No." I shake my head. "I'm not going to break."

He grins. "That's my girl." And in the next second he plows into me until he's fully seated.

His bigger than I thought. Thicker and longer.

I suck in a breath and freeze as my body accommodates his size.

He bites my earlobe.

"Give it a second, but only a second." He licks just below my ear. "Fuck, you feel so good, little bird. So fucking good." He slowly draws back, just until I think he's about to leave me, and then he thrusts forward again.

It's easier this time.

The third time is even better. And by the fourth thrust, I have my legs wrapped around his flanks.

"So tight," he growls as he continues to thrust into me.

"I'm sorry."

"Never be sorry." He bites my cheek, just a little, before he kisses me. "Never be sorry. Just be you." He kisses me as he thrusts harder and harder.

He lets go of my wrists and moves his hands to my hips, driving forward while yanking me back toward him. I press my feet to the mattress so I can buck up at him. Every time he draws back, it's agony until he thrusts forward again.

"Oh. Zack. Please." I dig my fingertips into his shoulders. His muscles work below my touch, so hard, and so thick.

"Please, what? Tell me what you need." He's breathless as he kisses my neck, my cheek. "I'll give you anything."

"Oh!" I tighten. My stomach trembles, along with my thighs.

"Yes, sweet girl. Unravel for me. Give yourself over to me." He bites down hard on my breast as he thrusts harder into me.

Again, there's screaming. Only this time, I know it's coming from me. My throat feels like it's going to split with the force of it. But it's nothing compared to the intensity of my orgasm ripping through my body. I can barely breathe. My mind blanks.

All I'm left with are waves of pleasure crashing into me, carrying me away, before leaving me limp on the shore.

"Fuck, baby, that was beautiful." He kisses my cheeks. "Pull your legs back a little."

I spread my legs more, taking him more fully. I'm tender but it's perfect.

"Oh fuck, yes, like that." He wraps his arms under me, cupping my shoulders.

He thrusts. And thrusts. And thrusts, until he finally stills, and a beastly roar escapes as he finds his own release.

I watch his face. His control slips, and pleasure twists his lips into a grin as he slowly finds his way back to me.

He touches the side of my face.

"Are you all right?"

"Never better." I reach up and bite his shoulder. "Are you all right?"

He flashes a lopsided grin. "No complaints."

He kisses me, a passionate kiss that leaves me wanting more touches, more caresses, more bites from him.

But he pulls away, looks down at me, at the mess of his cum sliding out of me.

"Are you on the pill?" he asks.

"No." I shrink back into myself. "I...I can't have children. What they did to me...I'm too broken inside."

His jaw sets.

"They will pay, Harley. For everything they did to you, your sister and your mother. They will all fucking pay." A more sincere vow, I've never heard.

"Good." I smile a little. Operating under the assumption they'd never be caught, never take any responsibility for what they did, has left me with as many scars on my soul as I have on my legs.

"It's almost morning." He slides next to me, pulling me to his side. I thought he was getting up to get a towel, but he pushes my legs back together, and nuzzles my hair.

"I like the idea of me drying on your skin," he says.

I smile into the dim room.

"I do too."

"Think you can sleep some more?" He pushes my hair behind my ear and kisses me just below my earlobe.

I yawn.

"I think so."

"Good. We have a busy day tomorrow and you need your rest."

"What are we doing tomorrow?"

"Monster hunting."

TEN

Zack

"Have you ever met a cop that didn't have a little dirt on them?" Jeff, my contact laughs on the other side of call.

"It's been a while since I saw a spotless one, yeah. What did you find on her?" I run the towel over my hair. Harley was still asleep when I got up, so I left her in bed while I showered and got dressed. The water pressure in this place is unacceptable. I'm going to fix that for her, too.

"Not a whole lot. FBI has more resources to cover up their shit. But I did get a listing of open cases Laurens is still listed on."

"Anything there?" I ask.

The shower kicks on in the bathroom. She's up. It's almost noon.

"Yeah. She's the lead on the Jessica Hamilton case."

"Really." I leave the towel on a chair and pull my bag onto a table. I find the file I had on Jessica and pull it out, flipping through the paperwork. "I don't see any FBI involvement with Jessica."

"It's active but not a priority. She works with the local department. If they get anything, they report to her."

"So, she's just there to babysit," I scoff.

"More than likely, she's there in case they actually get a sniff of something that could link Dustin to the case."

"Why would she care about Dustin?"

"Now that I see her on both these cases, Harley's and Jessica's, there might be some cross over. Let me dig a bit more. I'll get back to you.

I head to the bedroom to get a shirt.

"All right. I'm going to look more into Special Agent Laurens while you're doing that."

"Careful, Barns. Taking out some dirtbag who has this sort of rap sheet won't bring too much heat on you, but you go after an FBI agent and you're gonna bring down the full agency on you."

"When have you known me to act before I have all the information?" The shower turns off, and a moment later I hear her humming in the bathroom. I don't bother fighting the smile it brings me.

"When? Commander Smythe's tent." His voice dips.

"I wasn't wrong," I defend.

"No. You weren't. I'm just saying, let's get more information on her before you take her out. You can get the bigger fish." He has a point.

While I didn't mind taking out both my fucking C.O., and the Afghan commander who were sharing a young boy from the village, had I not killed them so quickly, I might have gotten information on which government officials were sanctioning such actions.

"Nothing final. Just gonna do some reconnaissance," I assure him. The bedroom door creaks open, and Harley steps out. Small droplets of water drip from her still wet hair onto the pink T-shirt she's paired with a pair of jeans cut off at the knee. They're just long enough to hide the pretty scars on her thighs.

I sink into the armchair in the living area as she makes her way toward me. Little peaks show through the T-shirt. My sweet girl isn't wearing a bra. When she reaches me, she climbs into my lap, straddling me.

"I gotta go. Get back in touch when you find that link." I hang up the call and toss the phone onto the couch.

"Anything important?" Her eyes follow the phone as it bounces on the cushion.

"Not yet." I grab her by her hips, pulling her into me, inhaling her vanilla bean shower scrub.

"You're not wearing a shirt." She leans back and runs her fingertip down my chest, stopping at a particularly ugly scar just above my left pec muscle. "What happened here?"

I look down at it, though I don't need to.

"A bullet, baby." I grab her wrist, bringing her palm to my lips.

"Who shot you?" Worry takes over her expression in an instant.

"Bad men. Real bad men." Leaning back, I let her get back to inspecting all of the marks on me. She traces the tattoos, one for every tour I did overseas.

"And this?" She runs her fingernail up the scar over my stomach. "This wasn't a bullet."

"No. A knife," I hiss when she digs her fingernail into the skin. It's been healed for five years, but the scar still has some sensitivity to it.

"I know this one." She pulls my arm up and brings the inside of my forearm to her mouth, pressing her lips to the largest tattoo on me. It features the wings of an eagle set behind a skull with fire in its eye sockets. Between the wings and the skull is a crossing of a Fairbairn-Sykes fighting knife and a sword. Flames and lightning bolts are set in the background.

"You do?" I brush a wet strand away from her face.

"Yeah. My uncle had one like it. Not exactly, but similar. You were a Marine?"

I pause. "I was."

"Special Forces...no, they call it something else." She scrunches her lips up while she's thinking, and it gives her the most innocent sex appeal. My cock hardens beneath her.

"Raiders. The unit is called Marine Raider Regiment." I wrap my arms around her ass, pulling her to me so I can kiss her throat. "Your uncle was a Raider?"

"Mmmhmm." She nods. "When he died, Mom had a full military funeral for him." She sinks further into my lap, moving her feet to curl around my back. "Are you still in the Marines?"

I laugh. "No. They politely asked me to leave five years ago."

"You were kicked out?" The look of shock on her face is cute, like she doesn't think I could do anything wrong.

"No." I shake my head. "I stopped some bad men from doing bad things to innocent kids. I was asked to keep quiet about it, and they asked me not to re-up for another tour."

Her brow wrinkles. "What bad things?"

I run my fingers over her forehead. "They won't do them anymore. I made sure of it." I wink.

She stares into my eyes like she's trying to get a grasp on me.

"You're a very dangerous man, aren't you?" She cups my cheek.

"I am, yes." I won't lie to her. No matter what, I will always tell her the truth. "But I'm not dangerous to you."

"Why?" She tilts her head to the right.

"Because you're good. And I'm only dangerous to the monsters of the world."

She smiles. "I like that."

"You do?" I chuckle.

"I do. There are a lot of monsters." She sighs.

I squeeze her hips.

"There are." I kiss her chin. "I want you to do something for me, if you think you can. If it's too hard, you have to promise to tell me." I harden my voice a fraction. I won't have her pretending with me. I need to trust she knows where her limits are.

"What is it?"

"Do you still have that FBI lady's card?"

"Yeah?"

"I want you to get a message to her that you've remembered something, and you want to talk to her. Tell her you want to meet her down at her office."

"But I haven't remembered anything."

"I know, but I want to talk to her."

She shrugs. "I don't think it will help, but sure."

She moves, like she's going to climb off my lap, but I hold her steady.

"Not yet, little bird." I work her thin T-shirt up her torso until her breasts are exposed and right in front of me.

She laughs. "What are you doing?"

"What I've wanted to do since you walked out here with your nipples peeking out of this little shirt." I lock eyes with her then lean in, taking a nipple between my teeth and biting down.

She hisses, and it's the most beautiful sound I've heard. I kiss the valley between her breasts and move to the other side, licking her, teasing the little nub into attention before clamping my teeth down on her.

"That feels...so good." She looks down at me.

"Take these shorts off, little bird." I slap her ass.

She jumps off my lap and I manage to get my own pants off before she's ready to climb back on.

"Wait," I order, pointing at her. "First, you pull your shirt up and tuck it between your teeth."

She chews on her lower lip. "Like a gag?"

"Does that scare you?" I ask.

Her cheeks flush. "I can take it out if I need to?"

"Of course." I nod. "You can just open your mouth and drop it."

"All right." She scrunches up the pink material and bites down on it.

"Good girl, now climb on, baby." I help her get settled, her legs on either side of me and lower her slowly onto my cock.

The moment her heat surrounds me, I groan.

"Fuck, you feel so good." I lean forward, taking a nipple in my mouth. This time I suck hard until she's moaning.

"Fuck me, Harley. Hard." I slap her ass while moving to the left side. "Your tits are so sweet. So fucking sweet." I suckle hard again, before biting down.

She's moving up and down my shaft, her muscles squeezing me with each movement.

I let go of her nipple, and bite down on her breast.

She sucks in an air, doubling her speed.

"Fuck."

The T-shirt soaks up her moan. Digging her fingers into my shoulders, she rides me faster, harder.

"Good girl." I slap her ass. "Harder." I slap her again.

"Make it hurt, Zack. Please," she begs, thrusting her chest at me. The shirt falls from her pretty lips with her plea.

I lick the tip of her nipple, smiling at the annoyance in her groan.

"No. Not like...oh, fuck, yes, like that!" She cries out when I bite down on her tit again, moving an inch, and biting harder.

She moves her feet, taking me even deeper, and I throw my head back, roaring my pleasure.

"Oh! I'm! Oh!" Her eyes fly open and, in another breath, she screams with her head thrown back. Her fingernails will leave marks in my skin, but I don't give a fuck.

I grab her hips, holding her steady while I pump upward

into her, again and again. Her body pulsates around me as her orgasm ebbs. I go harder, faster. Until my balls pull up tight, and I scream her name.

Little sparkles of light dance in my vision as my orgasm fades, and her smiling face comes into full focus.

"You were really loud," she laughs. "My neighbors might have heard you."

I grin.

I pat her ass. "Good."

ELEVEN

Harley

Special Agent Laurens is late. I check my phone again. She was supposed to be here twenty minutes ago.

"It's all right, Harley." Zack pats my hand across the table. Special Agent Laurens didn't want me going down to the field office, and it's over an hour's drive to her office in the city, so we found a spot halfway to meet.

"What if she thinks I'm lying?" I ask, leaning back against the hard back of the chair; it's one of those that are connected to the chair beside it and the table. The Rueben sandwich I ordered sits untouched in front of me.

"She won't. You need to eat something; you haven't eaten all day." He pushes the red plastic basket at me. His sandwich, ham and Swiss on rye, is nothing but crumbs in his basket. The homemade chips are all gone, too.

"I'm too nervous," I say, but I pick up a chip and nibble on the edge of it. "She's been nothing but nice. Why would you think she's not a good cop?"

He lifts a shoulder and wipes his hands on the paper napkin. "Even good apples can have a few bruises."

A ring of the bell over the front door draws my attention.

"It's her." I sit up straighter, taking a deep breath.

"It's all right. You remember what to say?" he asks, moving his things to my side of the table and sliding into the seat beside me.

"Harley. Hi." Special Agent Laurens smiles when she steps up to our table. I scoot out of the chair and greet her with a short hug. It's how I've always greeted her. Changing now would be weird.

"Hi. This is my friend, Zack." I gesture toward Zack who is watching her with an interested eye, but he schools his fierce expression into a warm grin.

"Hi. Nice to meet you." He stands up and offers his hand.

She shakes it, keeping her eyes trained on him. An FBI agent *has* to know when someone's lying to them.

How am I going to get through this without her calling me a liar?

"I'm sorry I'm so late. Traffic was heavier than I expected getting out of the city." She drops into the chair where Zack had been sitting.

"Not a problem. Do you want a sandwich?" Zack offers in the gentlest tone I've heard him use.

"No, no, thanks, though. I have to get back. It's a bit hectic. I hope it wasn't too much trouble meeting here." She smiles at me, folding her arms so her elbows lean on the table.

"No. No trouble," I assure her. "Thanks for taking the time. It's nothing mind blowing, but I thought you should know about it."

She nods.

"Of course. Anything you can remember would be helpful." Her eyes wander to Zack. "I assume she's told you about what happened?"

"She has." He lays his arm over the bench's back, behind me. "Horrible."

Special Agent Laurens nods. "It was." Her lips pinch together. "Whenever you're ready. Take your time."

I nod. We've been through this before. Usually, I have nothing for her, and we spend a few minutes talking over what's been done so far. Then we end it, and she leaves.

But today is different.

"The nightmares started up again a month ago." They never completely stop, they just leave me alone for a little while before thrusting their ugliness into my life again.

"All right." She leans forward, really paying attention. She's always given me the sense that, no matter what's happening around us, she's completely homed in on me. She never gets distracted by a phone call or some other conversation. I'm the only one she's listening to.

"Well, when I woke up from one the other night, I started thinking about things and..." I blow out a breath. Zack rubs my back with his hand. A simple touch that transfers his strength right into me.

"I remembered a name," I say. "Artie." The name pops out of my mouth before I can stop it.

Zack's hand freezes.

This isn't the information he wanted me to feed her. But it just came out.

"Artie?" Special Agent Laurens sits back in her chair. "Just that name?"

I nod. "Yeah. Just Artie."

She stares at me a long moment, her expression unreadable.

"I'm sorry. I know it's not much." My shoulders sag. It's too late now to tell her the lie I was supposed to tell her. It won't make sense, and she won't believe me.

"No. No it's good." She pulls her phone out and taps away on the screen. "A name is more than we had before." She smiles up at me. "I'm gonna make a note here, and then when I get back to the office, I can go through the file again. Maybe there's something there."

"Good." I glance at Zack. He's watching Laurens intently, but his hand has moved to my shoulder. He gives me a little squeeze.

"Did you talk to your mom about the name?" Laurens asks. "Did she remember it too?"

"No." How could I have? It only just came to me. "It's really hard this time of year for her. I didn't want to upset her more by bringing it up."

"I understand." She nods. "Maybe she mentioned it when everything first happened. If it's in the files, I'll let you know, and we can both talk to her at the same time."

"Yeah. That sounds like a good idea." I nod with relief. Calling Mom out of the blue with this information will only make things more difficult for her. She's been through so much, and this week is already bringing up all the horrors for her all over again.

"How is she, otherwise?"

"Oh. Good. She retired last year. She's good," I say. "I think she'll miss the kids when we go back at the end of August."

"That's right, you two taught at the same school, right?" she asks with a little laugh. "That had to be a little weird, after she'd been there for so long."

I shake my head a little. "No, not really. She liked having me there. Getting my teaching degree and then getting the job at her school really made her happy." I sit a little straighter. It had been important to her, and that made it important to me.

"And how about the two of you? How long have you been seeing each other?" she asks, still typing away on her phone.

"Not long," Zack admits.

She raises her eyes to his, her fingers still over the screen.

"You still live in the same apartment as last time we spoke?" She moves her eyes to me.

"Yeah." I nod, tucking my hands beneath my legs. I'm shaky all of a sudden. Her features haven't changed—she's still smiling slightly, and being friendly—but there's something darker about the way she's looking at me.

"Any big plans for the summer? You still teach elementary right, during the school year?" She finishes with the phone and tucks it away.

"No, no plans. Just working at the bar and relaxing a little before I go back in August."

She nods. "I still don't know how you can handle all those little kids." She forces a shiver and a laugh. "I'd take criminals over little ones any day."

Zack laughs, moving his arm from around me and pressing his forearms into the table.

"She's good at it though," he says firmly. There's no way he can know that, but it doesn't stop the pride from swelling in my chest.

"I'm sure." Laurens smiles a little wider, but her eyes are saying something else. I wish I could read people as well as Zack seems able to. "You still have my number, so if you think of anything else, you call me again."

She gets up from the table. "Talk soon." She smiles at me then hurries from the deli.

"She's quick. In and out, huh?" Zack watches her leave.

"She's always on a case," I say. "I'm sorry. I was going to say what you told me to say, but out of nowhere, that name just popped into my head."

"It's fine." He turns to me; his eyes soften when they meet mine. "It's true, though? The name you said, it's what you remember?"

"Yeah." I nod. "Like a bolt of lightning, just came out of nowhere. But it's true. I remember it."

"Good." He brushes my hair from my face. "Now eat your lunch. I'm gonna make a call and see if I can get any more information."

"Do you still work for the government?" I pop a chip into my mouth.

He leans over, kisses my temple. "Not really. I'll be right outside. Finish your lunch, or you'll get no dessert when we get home." A deep crease appears in his cheek when he grins and then he winks.

"I'll eat," I promise.

"Such a good little bird."

TWELVE

My sister cries beside me. Soft sobs, so not to draw the attention of the man sitting at the door.

He's in charge of watching us. To be sure we don't do anything other than eat, like we've been told.

We each have a bowl of oatmeal in our laps. I hate oatmeal, but it's the first bit of food they've given us since we woke up in this pit of hell. So, for the moment, it's my favorite dish.

"Eat," Mom chides my sister, but she's shaking her head. "You have to eat. You need strength, sweetie."

Her head is down and her hair blankets her face, so I can't see the bruising on her cheek. When they brought her back, she had more marks on her than before. Her eye is swollen now.

More blood dries on her legs. On the inside of her legs.

Rage builds in me, but I have to control it. I have to keep docile or they'll hurt her or Mom again. I have to stay calm, so they keep their attention on me. If I draw them to me, I can keep them both safe from more hurt.

"You got two minutes," the guy at the door yells.

"Hey, Artie!" A voice calls from across the expansive space. It's too dark to see anything clearly, but I can make out a form. "You got a phone call. I'll watch them."

"Shithead, don't use my fucking name!" Artie's chair hits the floor when he jumps up from it.

"Whatever, they won't tell anyone. Will you girls?" The sneer in his voice makes my stomach turn. "You got a call. In the office."

"They got one more minute to eat, then take that shit from them."

"How long you gonna play with them, anyway?"

"As long as fun can be had." Artie laughs. "Be right back."

A door opens and shuts. My sister jumps.

"Not gonna eat?" The man appears in front of me, sticking his finger into my oatmeal.

I raise my eyes up to him. He's not horrible to look at—clean-shaven, and his hair is swept back. He's wearing a business shirt and slacks.

"I hear you're the mouthy one. That right?" He grabs my chin, shoving his thumb into my mouth. "Feels nice and warm in there." He grins. "Maybe you'd be a better girl if you had something else to eat." He lets me go and rubs his crotch.

My sister whimpers.

"Leave her alone," Mom demands.

He looks over his shoulder at her.

"Is Mom jealous?" He laughs, taking my bowl of oatmeal and tossing it away from me. It clanks and splatters onto the floor. My stomach twists. I should have shoveled more of it in before he got here.

He twists my arm behind me and gets my wrists bound before moving over to Mom. He shoves her bowl out of her lap, and another rag into her mouth. She's completely gagged before he cuffs her hands, too.

When he looks at my sister, he chuckles.

"Fought too much, that one. But I think she learned her lesson," he says, moving back to me.

"Please. Just leave us alone," I say through gritted teeth.

Mom yells behind her gag, which only makes him laugh.

"I think she really is jealous. It would be cruel not to let her watch, right?" He winks at me, then shoves my shoulders. I fall backward, hitting the concrete floor hard.

I cry out from the pain.

He's over me again, straddling me. My wrists hurt from landing on them.

"Can't see well like this." He jerks on my arms until I'm lying sideways. Mom can see me, but I don't look at her. I can't.

He moves to my left side, leaving her on my right. I close my eyes, praying whatever he's going to do, he'll do it fast and then leave.

A zipper sounds.

Material shifts.

"Open up, girlie." He pats my cheek.

When I open my eyes, his hard dick hovers over my mouth.

I shake my head, but he slaps me harder. And when I still don't comply, he pulls out a knife.

"I can just cut off your fucking lips if you'd prefer." He presses the blade to my mouth.

I shake my head.

Fine.

I'll get through it. I've gotten through so much already.

As soon as I part my lips, he shoves his cock down my throat. I gag, choke, but he doesn't care.

He thrusts and thrusts. I try to turn away, but there's nowhere to go. He's over me, fucking my mouth as though it's just another hole.

I think to bite, but I know what will happen then. And he might do it to me.

"Fuck." He grunts as his thrusts get deeper. He angles his hips. I gag again. This monster won't care if I choke to death on my own vomit while he rapes my throat.

"Fuck yes." He pulls out just as he comes, and he jerks his cock, spilling his mess all over my face and neck. I gag, turning away as I throw up.

He laughs.

"See? Better than oatmeal, huh?" He pats my cheek, then drags my gag back up between my lips. It's soaked with his grossness.

Grabbing my shirt, he yanks me back up to seated. The salty taste of him sits on my tongue.

"Don't worry, Mom. Maybe next time," he says as he pulls the zipper back up on his pants.

I bring my tear-filled gaze up to my mom.

She's looking away.

The tears fall, mingling with the mess he made on me. The lights go out again. Now that we're bound, they don't need to watch us.

The door opens and shuts.

The silence deafens me.

THIRTEEN

Zack

Harley sleeps in her bed, with the bedsheets tangled around her thighs. She's animated in her sleep, tossing and turning most of the night. In all her moving around, she's repositioned herself diagonally across the bed.

If I were in it with her, I'd have her legs wrapped around me.

Not a bad way to sleep.

I kick my legs out from the chair I'm sitting in. I brought it from the kitchen so I could watch her sleep while I wait.

The red numbers on her alarm clock tell me it's two in the morning.

She finished her shift at the bar two hours ago, and has been asleep for the past hour. It's a wonder she falls asleep so quickly. The moment her eyes close, her breathing evens out and she's off to dreamland.

Tonight, I'm hoping it's all good dreams. But after what she came up with today, I'm not sure that's going to happen.

Jeff hasn't gotten back to me yet with what I want to know, but I can't be too pissed at him. He's got his own work to keep him busy, plus the bastard went and got married after he retired.

Looking at Harley, sleeping so soundly, I wonder if he *wasn't* completely off his rocker getting hitched. There's a profound innocence to her that I crave to protect, to keep locked up for myself, but it's more than that. Her strength is buried just below the surface, and I want to scratch until it emerges.

She survived the horrors of being kidnapped with her sister and mother and chained up for days. And while I can sense the guilt in her, for being the one who walked out of that place, she's never taken a single day for granted.

The woman has every reason to hide from the rest of the world, but she faces it every day. She may hate being around people, but I've met a lot of fucking people and she's not missing anything. But becoming a teacher? Being responsible for the education of a little kids, and being protective of her mother? She's got more grit than she thinks.

A click echoes in the deep silence, and I sit up in the chair. I check the windows in the bedroom—nothing there. Quietly, I stand up. Barefoot, I make no sound as I make my way through the apartment.

Another click stops me in the living room.

The deadbolt is being fucked with. I move to the side of the door, pulling my gun from my waistband.

I press my back against the wall, flush with the door. The bolt slides out of place and the door is shoved open.

The piss poor excuse for a chain lock actually keeps the door from opening all the way, but the fucker came prepared. A bolt-cutter slips through the opening and cuts the chain away.

I do one more check on the bedroom. She's still inside. The door's shut.

I pull back the slide on my Glock.

As the door opens, I slow my breath, waiting for the asshole to enter.

If it's the agent herself, she's going to be in a lot of fucking pain before I fucking kill her. I wouldn't mind being wrong.

Just this once.

But if I'm right, this isn't a wellness check.

The intruder is inside; he creeps into the living room. He's in head-to-toe black. Even his eyes are covered with a sheer covering.

As he steps inside, he looks around the room. All the lights are off. The window curtains are shut so the streetlights can't give him any advantage.

I lift my gun, pointing it at the back of his head. With a hard kick, I shove the door shut and it slams.

He freezes.

"Don't fucking move." But of course, the fucker isn't going to listen.

He flips around on me, spinning on his heel. Just as he faces me, I kick out, knocking his gun from his left hand.

"Fuck!" He launches at me, but I'm not new to a little hand-to-hand. I let him come at me. His shoulder hits my stomach, but I brace for it. Leaning over just enough, I wrap my arm around his torso, keeping him pinned in the bent over position as I run him through the apartment.

He trips on his own feet, and I let him fall to the floor on his back.

"Who the fuck are you?" I point my weapon at his face.

"Fuck you." He sneers up at me.

"All right then." I keep my gun trained on him while I step over him, opening the small box I left on the table, and taking out the injection I prepared.

A swift kick to his ribs keeps him down when he tries to get to his feet.

I throw my knee into his stomach as I kneel on him. Using my teeth, I yank off the cap of the needle.

"Who are you?" I ask again, holding the injection in my left hand now. Good thing about this drug, there's no need to be specific where it's injected. A leg muscle, a neck, chest, doesn't matter. So long as it goes under the skin, this fucker's gonna have a world of problems once it's in his system.

"I said. Fuck. You." He tries to grapple, but he's not as strong as me. Not as experienced with monsters as I am.

I jam the needle through his shirt, into his arm, and shove the plunger through the barrel, sending every drop of the liquid into his body.

"What the fuck!" he yells as the medicine makes its way into his tissue. It burns like a motherfucker. Right now, his skin feels like it's on fire. His insides are heating up, too.

He tries to lunge at me again, but the medicine works fast. There's no mobility in his muscles.

I sink back, sitting on his stomach as I catch my breath.

Fuck. I may need to start hitting the gym again. It's been a while since I had a good wrestle.

"Now." I lean over the prick, pressing my palms into the floor on either side of his head. "Who the fuck are you?" I yank off the black ski mask.

"What...did...." Each word is harder to get out. "You...do..." His head rolls to the side and he's out.

Well shit. I'd hoped to get at least one answer out of him before he passed out.

"Zack?" Harley's sweet, questioning voice hits me and I look up.

She's standing in the doorway of her bedroom. The oversized T-shirt she's wearing for a nightgown hits just above her thigh. Her hair's all messed up in a ponytail, and she's rubbing sleep from her eyes.

Fuck, the woman is gorgeous, no matter what time of day.

"What's going on? Who is that?" She steps into the room, pointing at the man asleep beneath me.

"I don't know yet." I climb off him and go to her.

Her brow wrinkles. "You're dressed already. Were you waiting for him?"

"I had a suspicion someone would be coming tonight; I didn't want to worry you."

"Did Agent Laurens send him?" She's sharp, this girl of mine. "To hurt me?"

"I was hoping I was wrong about her. We'll know for sure once we talk to him. But we can't do that here." Cupping her face, I pull her attention to me. "Go get dressed for me, all right?"

She nods.

"I can't make out his face. Do I know him?" She tries to lean toward him, but I get in her way.

"You'll get a better look when we get where we're going. Go get dressed now." I turn her toward the bedroom and send her on her way with a slap to her ass.

She looks over her shoulder. "Are we gonna hurt him?"

The woman knows exactly the way to my heart.

"Yeah, baby. We're gonna hurt him. But first, he has to answer some questions. No more questions from you, though. Go." I point to the door as I give the command.

She tucks her bottom lip between her teeth, trying to hide the smile playing on her lips, then does exactly what she wants to do.

She obeys.

FOURTEEN

Harley

My stomach flutters as we pull into a storage facility. It's one of those places that looks like a bunch of garages butted up against each other.

"Here we go." Zack drives right up to the last garage door in the row. It's three thirty in the morning, but the parking lot lamps are dead.

"Is he going to be able to talk?" I climb out of the car and meet Zack at the trunk where he's put the mystery man.

"Yeah. The sedative's probably already worn off. But he won't be able to move." He opens the trunk and there he is.

Fearful eyes land on me as the man looks up at us.

Dread rips through me, and I have to take a step back from the trunk. I need space from this man.

"What's wrong?" Zack turns to me.

I shake my head.

"I don't know. He's...I think I've seen him before." I swallow. "Do you need help with him?" I force myself forward. There can't be any hiding from what needs to happen. If I'm ever going to find out the truth of what happened to my sister, to find those responsible, I need to be brave. I can't let the anxiety and fear drown me.

"I got him, but can you open the door?" He hands me a ring of keys from his pocket. "The square one." He's already bending into the trunk, grabbing the guy.

The metal door bangs as I yank it up, and it rolls back on the tracks. Inside is a small space. The concrete floor is covered in thick plastic, and there' a chair in the middle of it. A toolbox sits on a card table.

"This is your place?" I ask him as he passes me, the guy draped over his shoulder.

"In a way." His voice is strained, but that's not surprising with the massive man weighing him down.

"In what way?" I draw the garage door back down until it slams shut. A shiver runs up my spine. Pulling my shoulders up to my ears, I try to block out the sound.

There's a grunt, then plastic rustles in the dark. A light turns on.

Zack's on me in the next second.

"Are you all right?" He cups my chin and drags my face toward him.

I swallow.

"Yeah. It's just…" I take a calming breath. "That sound. The garage door. The metal…it hurts." I tap my temple.

He glances at the man slumped forward in the chair.

"Do you want me to handle this? You can go to the car if you feel more comfortable."

I shake my head. "No. I'm fine." I take another deep breath. "It just startled me."

He searches my face, then gives a short nod. "All right, but if you need me take over, little bird, you tell me." There's a warning in his tone that sends warmth coursing through my veins.

My protector.

"I promise." I tug my chin from his grasp. "Let's get what we came for."

I walk behind him as we circle the man slumped in the chair. His arms dangle off to the sides and his chin is buried in his chest.

Zack grabs his hair, yanking his head back so we can see his face better.

Drool slides down his cheek.

"Gross." He looks half dead the way his face slouches.

"It's the drug. He's completely paralyzed from the neck down. But it makes the muscles of the face pretty numb too," Zack explains.

Faded blue eyes frantically search the space, and us.

"I think he's scared," I say, leaning over him a little.

"He should be." Zack laughs.

"Fuck." The man moves his jaw from side to side, like he's oiling a rusty joint.

"What's your name?" Zack leans over him with his hands pressing down on the man's shoulders.

"You're gonna kill me no matter what I say, so why would I tell you anything?" Our captive slurs his words. He's saying them right, and in the right order, but he sounds like he's drunk a few bottles of whiskey.

"Because." Zack moves behind him, turning our captive's head toward the card table. "Everything I need to draw this out for days is in that toolbox. And I know you don't want that. You want a quick death." He leaves his head hanging back against the chair. At least he's able to look at us now without dropping forward.

"People aren't going to just be okay with me dead. You're gonna be hunted down." It's hard to take the threat seriously when every word sounds like it's weighed down with an anchor.

"His wallet's in his back pocket." I point at the square bulge.

Zack smiles at me. "He can't be that stupid, can he?" He laughs, jerking the guy forward so he can get to the pocket.

He pulls out a leather billfold and flips it open.

"Fuck. He is." He shakes his head like he's disappointed. When he shoves the guy back to a sitting position, he frowns at him.

"You were supposed to be asleep. Easy kill," he says, his words getting easier to understand with each new sentence.

"But why?" Zack opens the wallet. Arthur Anderson," Zack reads the license inside.

I walk around to the front of Arthur, and he brings his eyes level with mine again. "Oh, god." I cover my mouth, jumping back from him.

"Oh. God." I suck in a breath.

"Harley." My name drops hard from Zack's mouth. "You're okay, little bird. Take a breath."

I suck in another breath.

"You." I point a finger at him, at the man who touched me, touched my sister. Who kept us bound for days, starving and thirsty and scared. Who took our mother away so we would have no comfort.

"Ah, I guess your memory really is coming back." He shakes his head. "Fucking shame."

I step up to him and slap him as hard as I can across his face. He tumbles out of the chair onto the plastic covering. He grunts, shakes his head.

"Good hit." Zack grabs hold of his arms and picks him up some sleeping toddler and shoves him back in the chair.

Once Artie is upright, Zack grabs his face and pushes it back.

"Laurens sent you?" he asks, but we already know. Who else would have done it?

"I'm not telling you shit." Artie's starting to get some of his bravado back. At least he's stopped drooling.

Zack throws a fist into his nose. Right after the crunch of cartilage breaking, blood spurts out.

Artie howls.

"Who does she work for?" Zack pulls a knife out from the holster beneath the leg of his jeans.

"Fuck off." Artie spits blood from his mouth. He's a dead man, and he knows it. Giving us information might speed up his death, but to his twisted mind, going out without becoming a rat gives him something to be proud of. Some sort of legacy.

Zack stabs the knife into Artie's thigh.

Artie howls. Tears fall while he bellows his pain.

"See." Zack yanks the knife back out and wipes it clean on Artie's black shirt. "You can't move, but you can still feel everything." He pats the flat of the blade against Artie's cheek.

"Artie. Artie!" I yell at him until he finally looks at me. "Who killed Quinn? Who was the other guy there that day?"

His sniffling turns to laughing.

"Just kill me." He shakes his head. "I'm not telling you anything. You don't understand. You can get rid of me, but it won't matter."

"Why? Why won't it matter?" I ask, panicked he's not going to give us any information. And we'll be no better off than yesterday.

Zack plunges the knife into his uninjured thigh, and Artie goes back to howling. Blood drips from his legs onto the plastic below.

"Who do you work for other than Laurens? Who else was there? Why were we picked?" I blurt out my questions, seeing how pale he's getting from the blood loss.

If Zack hit a major artery, Artie will pass out soon.

Artie stares at me for a long moment.

"You don't know how you got picked?" he asks with a twisted grin. "It wasn't random, I'll tell you that." He licks his teeth. "You were there on purpose."

Anger I've never felt before courses through me.

"Why would you want to hurt us? Why?"

"Your mom wasn't hurt," he argues.

"Who else is involved?" Zack demands, pressing the knife to his neck so hard, small pearls of blood appear. "Who brought the girls to you?"

"It was someone else. It wasn't you. Some other guys were there," I add so he knows I remember at least that much.

He shakes his head.

Zack moves the knife to his face and jams it into his cheek, dragging it up toward his ear. Blood pours down his face as he bellows with the pain.

"Dustin!" he finally yells. "It was Dustin Hastings," he spits the answer out when Zack brings the knife to his other cheek.

"And who else?" I push. It wasn't just one guy. I don't think. If the memories would just get clearer, I could be certain.

"Not positive." He rolls his gaze downward, like he's trying to see the tip of Zack's blade.

"And who the fuck do you work for?" Zack asks, the tip of the blade already cutting into his skin.

"I won't." He clamps his mouth shut even while Zack carves this side of his face.

There's a buzzing coming from the front pocket of Artie's sweatshirt.

"What's that?" Zack pulls his knife back and searches Artie's pockets. He pulls out a cell phone as it buzzes again.

"Got another for you, you got room?" Zack reads the message on the screen and looks up at Artie. "It's from Vince." He shows him the screen, but Artie's not paying much attention. He's still whimpering from the all the cutting.

I punch him in the thigh, right on the first stab wound. "He asked you a question. Who is Vince, and what is he talking about?" I shout in his ear.

Artie blinks while looking at me through tears and sweat.

Gone is the man with the wrinkled smiles and sadistic laughs. This man is sad. Pathetic. And he's not done paying for what he's done.

"You're...you're sick," he huffs.

"Who is Vince?" I ask again, softer this time.

"He's the guy you're looking for. He took Dustin with him that day. I don't know who else was there." He rolls his head to the side.

"Who does he work for?" Zack demands. "We need more names."

Vince.

I search my memory, but I don't find the name. Walking away from Artie, I pace behind Zack while he finds new piece of Artie to cut.

It's all there. In my mind, I know it is, but I can't reach it.

Fuck, this is annoying!

And Artie won't stop screaming. The sound proofing tiles on the walls soak up his cries, but it's like nails on a damn chalkboard to my brain.

"Zack." I tug on the back of his shirt. "He's not going to tell us anything else. We have his phone and a name." I see the fear in Artie's eyes. It has nothing to do with what we're doing to him, and everything to do with what will happen if he tells us.

Zack's shirt is covered in blood, his knuckles are drenched in it.

"You're right." He nods, pressing the tip of the knife to the man's throat.

"You hurt me. You hurt my sister," I say, reaching over to Zack's hand and covering it with my own.

Zack glances at me; pride fills his beautiful eyes. "Are you sure, little bird? There's no going back."

"He's a monster." I grip his hand. "And monsters need to be slain."

"That's right." He nods and turns back to Artie.

"No!" Artie cries out, but it's too late.

We're finished with him.

Together, we push the knife into his throat until the blade is completely in.

He gurgles, choking on the blood filling his throat.

Zack guides my hand, and we slice across hard, until his throat opens up, and blood pours out.

Pulling back, we let him fall to the floor. His blood pools around him as his head rolls to the side and all life drains from his eyes.

My heart beats against my eardrums, blocking out Zack. His mouth is moving. His eyes are drilled into mine, but I can't hear him over the thunder clapping in my ears.

I squat down and touch Artie's cheek. He's still warm, but there's nothing to him.

Any soul, as corrupt and wicked as it was, is gone.

"Harley." Zack's voice finally cracks through the noise, and I look up at him. His brows are knit together.

Slowly, I get back up and turn to him. Blood is on my fingertips. I rub them together.

He grabs my wrist and pulls my attention to him.

"Are you all right?" His question is so small. Am I all right? I smile.

"He hurt me," I say. "He hurt other people. And he didn't care."

He nods. "He was a monster, you were right."

I look down at Artie again. A limp little man is all that's left of the terror he was to me in those days, in all the years following. Nothing but a shriveled-up dead man.

"There are more out there," I say, barely above a whisper.

"Yes." A single word crashes down between us.

"We need to find them." I pull my hand from Zack's grasp.

I stare at his lips. His mouth is so full, so beautiful.

"We killed him," I say softly, waiting for the weight of guilt to crush me.

"We did." He brushes the back of his knuckles across my cheek.

"Am I evil?" I question. "This is the first time in years I've felt...well...normal. That has to be a bad thing, right?"

He shakes his head.

"No, Harley. Not at all." He cups my cheek. "You're taking back what they stole from you. You're not evil."

I draw in a shaky breath.

"You are so beautiful right now." He grins. "Like a light has flipped on inside you."

I nod. The knot in my chest has loosened. Breathing is easier.

Zack slips his fingers through mine, wipes the blood from my hand, and lifts his hand to my cheek.

Slowly, he smears the blood across my lips.

"Much better," he whispers then presses his mouth against mine.

His hand dives into my hair as he pushes me back against the cabinet, deepening the kiss. Through his jeans, his cock presses into my pelvis and I push my hips at him.

There's a hunger in me, and only he can feed it.

He tears my shirt off and shoves my pants down. I kick them away. His jeans are gone in a matter of a breath, and he has his cock in me.

"Oh, god. Oh!" I dig my fingernails into his shoulders as he pumps upward into me.

"So fucking good." He thrusts harder. I reach for him, kissing him hard as he plows into me.

We sink to the ground; he has me pinned and he's shoving my legs back. I roll my eyes back as his lips kiss down my collarbone, over my breasts.

I've never felt so alive.

"Harley," he mutters my name against my skin as he thrusts into me, his pelvis grinds into my clit. "So good."

My insides coil tighter.

His hand slides between our bodies and he rolls my clit beneath his fingertip.

"Such a good girl," he whispers in my ear as he bites down on my earlobe. "Such a good, good girl."

His praise courses through my veins like cocaine. My heart gallops, and my clit swells beneath his touch.

"Oh!" I arch my back, needing him, wanting him.

"Come for me, my little bird," he orders me and it's the authority, the confidence in his voice that's my undoing.

I scream as my body unravels, following his rule and exploding into a million pieces. I hope I never come back together.

"Such a good girl." He bites down on my neck, plowing harder and harder into me. Again and again, until he freezes. Arching his back, he lifts up as his own release carries him away.

I have never seen a more beautiful sight than these small moments when he loses his control.

Slowly, he comes back to me and lowers his mouth to mine. Gentle kisses now, soft, and yielding as he makes his way to my cheek.

"You're my perfect girl, Harley," he says, gingerly rolling away from me.

I smile. How can I not? I'm his perfect girl.

He collects my clothing and helps me get put back together.

"I suppose we need to take down this Dustin Hastings now," I say wiping my hands off on a rag Zack gives me.

"He can't help us," he says, sounding regretful.

I turn to him. "Why not? He helped Artie, and he might know who Vince is."

He frowns.

"Because I killed the fucker last week."

FIFTEEN

Zack

Harley sleeps like an angel, with her hair fanned out on the pillow behind her. She hasn't moved once since she fell asleep hours ago. It's as if a calm has settled over her soul.

My phone finally goes off, and I grab the call before it wakes her up. It's already noon, but last night was a lot for her. She needs her rest.

"Hey." I take my phone out of the bedroom and head into the living room. "What do you have for me?"

"Plenty. These assholes aren't doing a good job of hiding," Jeff starts.

"Maybe they don't need to. If they have a Special Agent on their payroll, no reason to believe they don't have more powerful people on there, too."

"That could be true."

"So what do you got?"

"Well, turns out Dustin and Artie were cousins. Couldn't find much on Dustin other than what we already knew."

"Who did he fucking work for?" I push the curtain away from the window enough to look down at the street.

"I'm getting to it. Damn, you're impatient today."

I pinch the bridge of my nose and take a deep breath. "It was a long ass night."

"All right, I'll get to it then. Artie has ties to the Blackwood family. Got busted a year ago with a tiny bit of product on him, and the Blackwoods sent their best attorneys to get him out of the jam," he says.

"They sent high-powered attorneys down for a drug dealer?"

"Yeah, seems overkill, right? I'm thinking Artie wasn't just a low-level dealer. Especially if he was sent last night to take you and the girl out."

My jaw clenches. "I didn't realize the Blackwoods had dealings in Chicago. I thought they stayed on the east coast."

"Nah. Jimmy is the youngest of the brood. He broke away from New York a long time ago. He's been in Chicago for the last fifteen years. But he's not peddling just coke."

"He's the loan shark of the family, isn't he?" Fucking Mafia families have their hands all over the fucking country. So long as they stick to shit that doesn't involve the innocent, I leave them alone. There are bigger monsters.

"That's where he got his start." There's a crackling on the line.

"And Vince? The phone number I gave you?"

"Yeah, that's what I mean when I say they're not hiding. It's listed to a Vince Scaletto. His rap sheet is a little more... disturbing. He spent five years in max security for multiple rapes– not all women, and not all adults. They tried to get him on trafficking, but nothing stuck."

"Only five years?" Even the most corrupt judge would have a hard time giving that little of a sentence to those charges.

"Yeah, those Blackwood attorneys were able to get the conviction overturned."

"Everything leads back to Jimmy Blackwood, then."

"In the end, yeah."

"Well, we'll pay him a visit after we speak to Vince." Taking a Mafia son out will need more finesse than one of his low-level thugs. He'll have people surrounding him, and possibly force of his family behind him.

It doesn't let him off the hook, it just means we need to watch our steps.

There's more static on the line, like it's fading out.

"Phone's gonna die on me. These prepaids are getting shittier," Jeff complains.

I chuckle. "They are when you go cheap."

"I'm saving for retirement. Not all of us get field bonuses."

"You couldn't stomach what I do. Besides, you have that wife and kid to protect. You're fine right where you are." There's movement behind me.

Harley is up, finally, brushing her hair from her face as she walks into the living room with a sleepy smile on her lips.

"You're right." More static. "If I get more, I'll get in touch."

"Thanks," I say to a dead line. He really needs to pay better attention to the equipment he uses.

"Who was that?" Harley pulls her hair into a ponytail as she makes her way to the kitchen. I don't miss the way her hips sway as she walks. Or the gentle curve of her ass that peeks out from her pajama shorts.

"A friend, getting information for us." I toss my phone onto the side table next to the couch on my way to meet her in the kitchen.

I slink my arms around her waist while she drops a coffee pod into her coffee machine, and kiss her bare shoulder.

"Sleep okay?"

"Yeah." She freezes. "I did." After hitting the brew button, she turns in my arms and faces me. "Not a single nightmare."

"Were you expecting one?" Taking out Artie was her first kill. He deserved every ounce of pain he got, but Harley's not the monster he was. It wouldn't be surprising if she'd found it hard to sleep.

"I was." She nods, pressing her palms into the edge of the counter. "After yesterday, I thought I'd be up the rest of the night with them. But nothing."

I brush an errant hair from her cheek.

"How are you doing? With what we found out yesterday?"

She lifts a shoulder, but her eyes move away from mine.

I nudge her chin until she's focused on me again. "No lying, Harley. Tell me."

She frowns. "We didn't find out much. I still don't understand why and who, other than that Vince guy."

"I was able to track down that Vince guy, well at least his last name. I have a little more digging to do, but I think I'll know where we can find him soon enough. Then we'll get more from him. It's slow, but one monster at a time, right?"

The little wrinkles around her eyes deepen with her smile.

"Yeah. One bite at a time." She laughs. "That's what I tell my kids when they're learning something new. You wouldn't eat a bear all in one bite, right? No, you'd eat it one bite at a time, so that's how we do the lesson."

"Why would you eat a bear?" I ask.

She thinks about it, then shrugs. "I don't know, none of the kids have ever asked."

"Probably because they trust you." I push back from her and open the fridge, grabbing the half-and-half for her. "Just like you trust me."

"I do." She nods. "It's weird, right? Feeling this connected to someone this fast? It's not normal. Maybe I am sick, like Artie said."

"The world is a sick and fucked up place, Harley. You're not the sickness." I hand her the half-and-half as the coffee sputters the last bit of brew into her mug. "You're going to be part of the cure."

"You killed Dustin. Is that what brought you to town? Him?"

"Yes." I nod.

"Why'd you kill him?" She pours the cream into her coffee while stirring in a heaping spoon of sugar.

"He was a bad man doing bad things."

"Why won't you tell me?" She drops her spoon into the sink.

"Because I like it when you sleep without nightmares."

She looks over her shoulder at me. "Don't start acting like I'm a fragile piece of glass. Not after what I did yesterday."

My eyebrows shoot up. "Fragile glass? You? Never."

"Isn't that why you call me your little bird? You think I'm a little innocent creature that needs to be protected in a cage?" She brings the mug to her lips and takes a small sip.

"No. I call you my little bird because you've just found your wings and are learning to fly."

She smiles. "I think I like that." She pauses. "But I still want to know what he did."

"If I tell you that it's better you don't know, you need to trust me."

She levels me with a stare, like she's considering what I'm saying.

"I do trust you, Zack." She nods. "But I'm tired of having things hidden from me."

"I get that." And I do. I spent over a decade serving in one of the top-tier special operations battalions in the Marines. I've seen things that would make Harley never sleep again, but I always believed we were the heroes. We were the good guys. But in the end, it was just bullshit.

We were fed lies to keep us going on missions, while the corrupt bastards back in their tents provided those that were considered trusted allies with innocents to abuse. All the while, we were made to stand guard, to hear their cries and do nothing.

Some fucking heroes we were.

"So you'll tell me?" She edges toward me with a coy smile.

I chuckle.

"I'll tell you this. He hurt a girl. He did things to her that were unforgivable, and for no other reason than he enjoyed it. I killed him because he was a monster."

"And all monsters need to be slain," she says.

"Yes."

"But we're not monsters?"

"No." I rest my hands on her hips, pulling her closer to me, and kissing her softly. "We get rid of the monsters."

She smiles after I pull back.

"So now we find Vince? What about Special Agent Laurens? She's going to realize Artie messed up, and she might send more guys." She takes another sip of her coffee and puts the mug down on the counter.

"I sent her a text from Artie's phone, telling her all went as planned. I'll watch for any messages from her on his phone, make sure she's not looking for him."

She hops up onto the counter and spreads her legs, giving me room to step between them.

"You've thought of everything." She rests her arms on my shoulders, running her fingers through my hair. It's so casual. So normal, these little touches.

A warmth I'm not used to runs through me, and I lean into her hands. "Have I?" I kiss her cheek, then her neck.

"Yeah." She tenses. "Were you this methodical in the military?"

"I was."

"And they didn't want you to stay?"

"No, baby." I kiss her cheek. "They didn't like how I got rid of bad guys."

Her eyes narrow. "But you were a soldier. Didn't you do what they trained you to do?"

I shake my head.

"Not always. I wouldn't let them get away with hurting people who didn't deserve it. That's why I got out." A medical discharge, instead of a court-martial, because they didn't want the publicity that would go along with the trial. Killing an Afghan commander while he was balls deep in a fourteen-year-old boy wouldn't have been a good look for us. Our own commanding officer had brought him to the tent, and that would have been bad for relations.

"Okay. So, we find Vince." She sighs. "Then what?"

I line up my eyes with hers and smile.

"We kill him, little bird. We kill him."

SIXTEEN

Harley

"Are you sure it's okay? Us being out?" I ask, while gesturing to the next street for Zack to make his turn.

"It's fine. I have it handled," he assures me again, and I trust him. It's been so long since I met someone and didn't second guess their motives or their words. What Zack says is what he means.

"Okay." I sigh. "She's the last house on the right."

Mom's outside, watering the rose garden Dad put in when I was a kid. She's wearing a wide-brimmed hat, and has on her gardening gloves. She must have been weeding; the knees of her denim capris have green spots on them.

She turns off the hose when she sees us climb out of Zack's car and turns a bright smile at me.

"Harley." She plucks off her gloves. "I wasn't expecting you, honey." She hugs me and kisses my left cheek.

"Sorry. I tried calling, but you must have been out here already." I gesture to the garden. "The roses are looking good this year."

She sighs, like keeping up with them is a heavy burden.

"They are. Your dad would be happy." She turns to Zack. "And who's this?" She lifts her left eyebrow at me.

"This is Zack." I link my arm through his.

"Well. Hello, Zack." Mom offers her hand with a smile, and he takes it.

"Nice to meet you, Mrs. Turner." He turns his attention to the garden. The front of the house is reserved for roses, and she's done an amazing job keeping what Dad planted and adding even more. It really is beautiful. "You definitely have a green thumb."

She laughs.

"I'm a forced gardener. I only keep this up because it would have made my husband happy." Her smile twitches a little on the edges. "What are you two up to today?" She asks.

"You messaged me yesterday about the upstairs toilet running. Did you get it fixed?" I ask.

"Oh. No, but you didn't have run over here for that. It can wait, I don't go up there that often." She gathers up the bucket of weeds and the small shovel. "But since you're here." She grins and leads us into the house.

After dropping her things in the mudroom just off the front entrance, we climb the short set of stairs to the living room.

"I'm gonna wash up real quick." She disappears into the bathroom.

"Thanks for coming with me, it will only take a second. I bet the chain's just wrapped around the thingy again," I tell Zack.

He smiles at me, like he's amused. "The thingy?"

"Yes." I nod. "The thingy."

"All right." She's back, and she's brought three bottles of water. Zack and I both take one, but neither of us opens it.

"Your picture is crooked, mind if I fix it?" Zack points to the family portrait hanging on the wall over the television.

She tenses but gives an abrupt nod. "I was dusting this morning," she explains.

He reaches over the television, mindful of the small basket of flowers there, and pushes the left side of the frame up until it's level again.

"It's a nice photograph." He steps back. I catch my mother's eyes lingering on him before moving to the photo.

"It was taken a year before my husband passed." She puts her water down and joins him, pointing at my father. "Richard was diagnosed with lung cancer a week after we took it."

My heart aches with the memories of my father's illness.

"It must have been a horrible time for you all," Zack says softly.

She raises her chin. "It was. He was very ill for a long time. None of the treatments worked." She slips her hands into her back pockets, making her elbows stick out. "We spent every last penny we had trying to make him better, and then some." She sighs.

"Dad lost his job and his health insurance, so a lot of the bills piled up." I lean back on the couch.

"Harley was a good nurse though." She looks over her shoulder at me. "He could always count on his little Harley."

Zack's shoulders lift.

Maybe it's her tone. Sometimes there's a touch of bitterness in it, but she doesn't mean anything by it. Sometimes the memories mix together with the pain, and it colors her tone.

"A bit of a daddy's girl, was she?" Zack smiles at her, and from his profile I notice a deep crinkling around his eyes. It makes him look more distinguished.

"She was definitely his favorite."

"Dad didn't have a favorite," I interject. "He was just as close to Quinn."

My mother's body goes rigid at the sound of my sister's name. An ache builds in my chest. I've triggered a deep pain.

"He wasn't. And you know it." She turns enough for me to

see her deep-set frown. In a blink, it's gone. "Wow, it must be warmer outside than I thought." She touches her forehead, like the heat is the reason for the bite in her words.

"It's supposed to be pretty humid tonight, too," I say. Talking about Dad and Quinn stirs up a lot for her and seeing her in pain makes me ache to fix it. She's been through so much, and she's done everything she could to protect me from the horrors of our past.

"I'll make sure to turn the air down then. You know I can't sleep if I'm too hot." She smiles, then reaches over and pats my arm. "Since you're here, mind checking that toilet?"

"Of course. That's why I stopped by." I put the water bottle down on a coaster with a smile. If I can project enough normalcy, maybe it will finally stick. A mom asking a daughter for a favor, can't be more normal than that.

"Think I need my tools from the car?" Zack asks.

"No. It's the thingy, I told you." I smile at him as we walk through the dining room to the stairs leading up to the second floor.

"Quinn and I had separate rooms up here, with a shared bathroom. Mom and Dad's room is downstairs, just off the living room," I explain as we step off the stairs into the small upstairs foyer.

"My room is on the left, her room was the right, and the bathroom's right there." I take short steps forward to the closed door and push it open.

The phone rings from my old bedroom. I like to tease Mom that she has the last landline in Chicago.

Mom's right, the toilet is running. After lifting the lid of the tank, I find the problem and untangle the thin chain. Problem solved. "See. The little thingy." I turn around with a wide smile, but Zack's not behind me. He's pushed the door to my old bedroom open to step inside, and my mother's voice carries out from inside.

"I don't know what you're talking about." Her voice is

sharp, coming through the answering machine still attached to the phone I had in my room as a teenager.

I lean against the doorframe of my bedroom. She hasn't touched it since I moved out after college. And she never let me change it during high school. After Quinn was gone, she wanted everything in the house to stay still. Unchanging.

The therapist she dragged me to suggested the familiarity might be good in order to get my memory back. And Mom did anything the doctors told her would help me.

Even while going through the worst event of her life, and dealing with guilt, and pain, and horror, she was always there, carrying around a safety net beneath me. If I fell, Mom was there to catch me.

Sometimes, realizing how horrible it was for her makes my own guilt worse. But I can't tell her that. I won't be the cause of any more of her pain.

"Mrs. Turner. After your daughter's death, you managed to pay off all of your debts. It totaled well above three-hundred thousand dollars," the caller on the other end of the line says.

"Well," my mom scoffs. "The community came together to help me. There were donations."

"Yes, I found that in my research. But the donations weren't enough to pay—"

"Why can't you leave us alone? My daughter was murdered for Christ's sake! And you want to dig it all up again? Just leave us alone!" my mother yells and slams the phone down.

I bring my gaze to Zack, who's watching me.

"I fixed the toilet." I turn away from the room. He follows me out, shutting my door quietly and crossing the small hallway to Quinn's room.

"Zack, wait." I try to stop him, but he's already inside.

I step in behind him.

My heart aches at the scene.

She's done nothing in here.

The bedding Quinn slept on is still on the unmade bed. A rocking chair is the only addition to the room.

"Mom sits in here sometimes," I say, lightly pushing the rocking chair until it starts to move. It creaks as it sways.

"She's kept it clean." Zack wipes a finger over the dresser.

"Harley?" Mom drops my name behind me like a hammer through the wood flooring. "Honey, what are you doing in Quinn's room?" She hurries inside and steps in front of Zack, who is standing next to Quinn's desk. Her journal sits opened to the last page she was writing on.

"Who was on the phone?" I ask. She's distracted with us being in this holy place, she might actually give me the truth.

"A reporter. Please. please, get out." She spreads her arms and shoos us from the room.

Once in the hallway she pulls the door closed, leans her forehead against it, and closes her eyes. We've tainted the room for her.

"What reporter?"

She spins around, pressing her back to the door, as though to protect the precious space from us.

"You know how they get this time of year." Her pale blue eyes land on me.

I nod. "I do. I'm sorry, Mom."

She takes a deep breath and pushes on a brave front. I've seen her do this so many times over the years, it's not really necessary anymore.

"Did you fix the toilet?" She moves to the bathroom and leans in. "Thank you, hun."

"No problem. It was just the chain. Do you want me to show you again?" I offer, but she shakes her head.

"That's fine. Thank you." She leads us to the stairs, and I nod my head for Zack to follow her.

Once we're back in the living room, I sit on the couch, Zack next to me while Mom takes the recliner facing us. She fidgets with her hands. We must have really unsettled her by going into Quinn's room.

"I saw Special Agent Laurens yesterday," I blurt out before I can find a tactful way of saying it. But since she's already on edge, might as well get it over with.

Now that memories are coming back, I could use her help to sort them in the right order. Zack also wants to be sure she's protected.

If Special Agent Laurens is as dirty as we think she is, Mom could be in danger, too.

"Why would you see her?" The question drops like a bowling ball between us, but she recovers quickly and pushes on a gentle smile. "I'm sorry. It's just I thought she stopped working on the case."

"Well." I take deep breath. "I remembered something, Mom. A name. Actually a few things, really, but the name came first." I squeeze my knees. "Artie Anderson. And another name, Vince."

Her jaw clenches, but it's so faint, I'm not really sure I saw it.

"Artie Anderson?" She shakes her head. "I don't remember anyone by that name."

"He's the one who held us in the…" I stop. Fuck this is hard. And I know I'm cutting into a barely healed wound for her. "He was the one who held us wherever we were held."

"They never figured out where we were kept, Harley," she reminds me. We weren't found by the police. We'd been dumped at our local hospital, unconscious. Quinn's body was dumped, too. It'd been washed completely of any traces of any evidence. Not a shred of evidence on any of us was found.

"I know, but I remember. It was dark, I remember that. And you weren't with us for most of the time. I remembered that, too." I start talking fast, now, as the memories start to uncover themselves. "And there was a lot of metal-on-metal sounds. I thought it was just the door, but I think maybe there were cars around us? Oil? Maybe gasoline? Something like that I remember smelling."

I take a breath. It's all starting to get clearer.

"Harley," my mom whispers my name.

I hadn't realized I stood up. I'm standing over her.

Slowly, I sink back onto the couch. Zack puts his hand on my knee. A comforting touch that grounds me.

"You told Special Agent Laurens all of this?" She asks softly, like she's worried.

"No, just the name. Everything else started coming after I spoke with her." I force my shoulders to relax. "I know it's hard, and with the...I'm sorry, Mom."

Zack squeezes my knee.

"It's really hard, I'm sure for both of you," Zack says quietly, drawing her out as she tries to fold into herself.

"You're not trying to find him, are you?" She asks me, leaning forward. "You can't go poking around this, Harley. It's not safe. Honey, I don't want anything to happen to you." She swallows. "You're all I have left. I can't lose you too." Her voice cracks with her worry.

"Why isn't it safe?" I ask. "Do you remember that name? Or what Vince looked like? Do you?"

She shakes her head. "Please." Jumping up from the recliner she paces the room. "Harley. We can't do this. Honey, we have to move on. We have to accept what happened, and just move on."

"But don't you want them to pay for it?" I push. "I mean, they made you–" my words cut short when her eyes snap to me. Fear trembles her.

"Please, promise me you'll let this go. Don't go poking." She glares down at me, and I haven't seen her this angry since the night I snuck back into the house after sneaking out in high school through Quinn's bedroom window.

"All right, Mom." I get up from the couch and make my way to her. "I'm sorry. I shouldn't have brought it up, I'm sorry." I haven't just scratched a wound, I think I've made a new one. "I'm sorry, Mom," I whisper.

Her bottom lip trembles.

"I'm not sure the memories coming back are a good thing, Harley. It's a lot to remember, to sort through. It's going to be like going through it all over again."

She's not wrong, but at least the fog will be gone. I will at least see the demons I've been fighting.

"Promise me you'll stop." Her hands are cold when she grabs mine. "Please, honey. I don't want you to go through all that again."

"All right, Mom. I promise." The fear rolls off of her, surrounds me.

She searches my eyes. I've never been able to lie to her, she can always sense it.

"I will stop," I say more firmly.

"Good." She drops my hands, sucks in a deep breath. "Now. If you don't mind. I think I need to lie down for a bit." She touches her forehead again.

"Yeah, Mom. Of course," I say, glancing at Zack. He's stayed out of our interaction, but he's been mentally making notes. I can see it in his expression. He has a definite opinion, and a dark spot in my gut tells me I'm not going to like it.

"Zack, it was nice meeting you. I hope you'll come back again some other time, and we can have dinner." Her manners will always overrule her emotions. Being rude to a guest just won't do.

"Of course." He stands up and inclines his head.

She flashes a fake smile, then heads to her bedroom, silently shutting the door behind herself.

"Let's go." He gestures to the front door. "She needs to sleep."

I climb down the front steps onto the lawn and turn back at the house.

"She's never gotten that upset before. I mean it always

upsets her if we talk about what happened, about Quinn. But this was different. She was panicked."

He nods.

"I made it harder." I turn toward the stairs. "I need to make it better."

"She's all right, Harley. She just needs to rest." He stops me.

I look back at the house, then at him. He's right. I know he is.

"C'mon let's get in the car." He leads me to the car, opening my door for me before rounding the front and getting in on his side.

"What's wrong?" I ask when he throws the car into drive and peels away from her house. "You look like something's wrong."

"Let me do a little digging before I say, all right? Until I know for sure?" He shifts gears and turns down a main road.

"All right." I settle into my seat. "I can do that."

He pets my leg. "Good girl."

And with two words, my heart stops racing and my mind quiets.

SEVENTEEN

Zack

People lie, but numbers never do.

My back muscles tighten as I scroll through the last bit of bank statements.

A whole hell of a lot of money fell into their accounts and then rolled right out. They were on the brink of complete financial ruin. The mortgage already had been borrowed against, four credit cards all maxed out, and in her name. Fuck, they didn't even own the family car, and the payments were months behind.

And then. Snap. All fixed.

"Fuck." I shove my laptop across the kitchen table, wishing the numbers would change.

A faint ding from my phone catches my attention, and I'm more than willing to be distracted.

Just at the grocery store. Forgot to pick up bananas.

A smile tugs hard on my lips as I read Harley's text. Such a normal message. Going to the store. I lean back in the chair and cradle the device in my hands while typing out a response.

Great. See you soon. Be careful.

Artie's phone vibrates on the table. It's been quiet since last night.

When I turn it over and see the notification that a text from Laurens has come through, my blood heats.

Why did I just get a call telling me Harley Turner is still breathing?

The chair flies back when I shove out of it. I had my suspicion. After the phone call from the reporter, then pushing Harley to drop the whole thing.

Something wasn't right.

Now she's got Vince's name too? Where are you?

I clench my teeth, grab my phone, and text Harley to come straight home after the store. We're going to have to speed up our visit to Vince. I'm still waiting to hear from Jeff on where I can find him, but staying here at her apartment isn't safe anymore.

Working on it.

I'm not sure my vague text will satisfy Laurens or not. If she's smart, she'll send reinforcements here to see if Harley's still alive and kicking.

And I'll fucking kill that fucker too.

Anyone so much as gives her a fucking shiver is going in the ground.

I can't explain this protectiveness I have for her. But I would burn the fucking world to ashes to keep her safe.

And, if this list of assholes gets much longer, it might be the whole city of Chicago that needs to go up in flames.

Meet tonight. 8 at the usual spot.

Well, that's not going to work.

I scroll through their past communications quickly, picking on any coding they may have used. None, because Artie was a fucking idiot.

Got it.

I text his usual response when she beckons him and drop

the phone on the table. I need to get Jeff on the phone and get a bag packed for Harley.

She can't tell her mom, either. And how am I going to tell her that?

How can I break her this way, telling her I'm not certain her mother can be trusted?

Maybe it has something to do with that new pension payment she's getting? From what I could tell, Richard Turner didn't have any pension with his company when he was let go.

So where did the money that dug her out of her hole ten years ago come from, and where is this money coming from now?

Be there two minutes. Something wrong?

I quickly text Harley back there's nothing to worry about, and then sit back at the table. Closing out the bank statements for Nancy Turner, I dive into the financials for Vince Scaletto.

Jeff was spot on. This man makes no attempt to hide his tracks, which makes me wonder what he actually does hide. If everything is so open book, it could be a smoke screen for the worst of it.

A quick scan, and I find his local hangout. Cuffs, a bar on the northwest side of Chicago. A divey looking place from the web pictures, but I'm sure that's a front. There's probably a whole back room full of money opportunities.

He can keep those secrets.

The credit card statements tell me where he likes to hang, but not when. We won't be able to have the sort of conversation we need to have at Cuffs.

"Hey. Everything all right?" Harley breezes into the apartment, several grocery bags in her hands.

"Yeah." I get up immediately. "You should have said you needed help." I frown at the bags.

"I'm not used to having someone here to help me. It's not bad. The cans were a little heavy." She opens the first bag and starts taking out the vegetables. "I wasn't sure what you liked, so I grabbed some apples and strawberries, and there're some chips in that bag over there."

I stop her before she starts putting things away.

"Don't bother unpacking them. We have to leave. I have somewhere else we can stay."

Her brow furrows with confusion. "You said everything is fine."

"It is for now, but Agent Laurens knows Artie failed last night."

"Already?" She puts the cans of black beans back on the counter and presses her hip against it.

"Yes."

"How?"

I bring her Artie's phone and wait while she scrolls through the texts Laurens sent. Her jaw tenses as she reads and when she brings her eyes back to mine, there's a mixture of anger and fear in them.

"You think Mom told her?" She hands me back the phone.

"She's the only one who knew you had talked to Laurens and that you were starting to get your memory back," I point out, hoping to ease her to the horrible conclusion.

"Well, maybe she wanted to check with her about the case. Maybe she wanted to see if she was going to be following up on the lead with the new name." She makes excuses for her mother, and I can't even blame her. If my mother was alive, if I had family that shared such horrors with me, I would want them protected.

But it's all formed pretty neatly in my mind. Though eyes looking from the outside tend to see more clearly than those within the trauma.

"You think Mom had something to do with it?" She slams the phone onto the counter. "You think she did something to cause us to be kidnapped? My sister killed right in front of me?" Her voice rises with each question.

"I don't know what her involvement is, but there are things

that don't make sense. After your father passed away, she was given a lot of money, Harley. Half a million dollars."

"She said Dad had an insurance policy; it was probably that." She's grasping at straws.

"No. It wasn't. Neither of them had life insurance policies. There's no record of one. There are only random deposits that add up to half a million dollars. And it covered almost all of the medical bills, plus the credit card bills that were maxed from paying doctors after your dad lost his job."

"I'm not listening to this." She covers her ears and closes her eyes. "Mom was there. She was taken, too. And then she... she had to make the worst decision. They weren't going to let us go. She had to make the decision, or they were just going to keep hurting us."

I pull her hands away from her ears easily and wait until she settles her eyes on mine. Her face is flushed with anger, and her eyes wild with fear.

"Who is 'they?' Vince and Artie?" I ask.

"No. I mean, I remember them, but there was someone else. There was a third guy, and he was the one who did it."

"Did what?" I'm pushing her now, but her frustration seems to be clearing up the cobwebs in her memory.

"He hurt us. Me and Quinn. And then he said time was up." Tears fill her eyes, glistening before rolling down her cheeks. "He pulled out his gun. He always had it tucked into his waistband in the back, like he was some gangster on TV."

I wipe away her tears. "Then what, baby? What happened then?"

"He put the gun to my head, then Quinn's, told my mom she had to choose. If she wouldn't, they'd just keep going on like they were. That they'd start using our..." she cuts off, a sob cracking through her. "They would start raping our assholes next."

Artie died too easily. Dustin didn't get enough payback

before he went, too, but Vincent? Fuck, am I going to make that fucker pay.

"He said, they'd bring in more guys and sell us like whores. And she'd have to watch. She had to choose, they said."

"Okay." I try to pull her in for a hug. Her breathing is getting erratic, her heartbeat throbs in the vein on her neck.

"They made her."

"Harley, take a breath."

She shoves my arms away and takes three long strides away before turning back to me. New tears are filling her eyes.

"He said 'Which is it?'" She swallows. "And she looked at us both, whispered 'I'm sorry...'" She slaps her hand over her mouth. "And she said my name. A second later, he shot Quinn in the head. Oh, god!" She doubles over, wrapping her arms around her waist, like the pain is too much.

"All right. Okay," I reach for her, needing to pull her into me, to absorb her pain. I can take it in like a sponge, she doesn't deserve it. She shouldn't have this sort of darkness touching her soul.

"No, Zack," she sobs, falling to her knees. In a heartbeat, I'm on the floor with her, pulling her into my embrace. She sucks in air, trying to fill her lungs.

"She wasn't choosing me to survive. She chose me to die."

EIGHTEEN

Harley

The room is dark when I wake up. We're not at my apartment anymore. Zack packed for me, and when I was ready, he walked me down to his car and we left my place, my life, behind.

I can't go back there.

Not ever.

I don't even want to be in the state.

I roll over in this massive bed and curl my knees up to my chin. I've never been so comfortable while feeling this miserable before.

Zack drove us over an hour away from home, to the city. We're in a building with a doorman. The elevator needed a security code to get us up to the apartment. Only in movies have I seen such luxury.

I don't know how he got this place for us, and I'm not sure I want to ask.

Blinking the sleep from my eyes, I push myself up to sit against the headboard.

My head feels like it was used to bowl a perfect game last

night. It goes well with the burning and dryness of my eyeballs.

Crying gives me the worst hangovers.

I grab my phone from the nightstand where Zack left it for me while he's out.

There are two messages. One is from Zack.

Don't open the door for anyone, little bird. I'll be home soon.

And one is from my mom.

Hey, hun, thanks for your help yesterday. That Zack guy is pretty cute. Where'd you say you met him? Anyway, I thought we could meet up for lunch tomorrow?

I stare at my mom's message.

Lunch. She wants to have lunch.

Anger rolls through me, and I drop the phone onto the bed, shoving it away from me.

Ten years. I've spent the last ten years weighed down by guilt over my mother picking me instead of Quinn. I'd felt like I may as well have been the one who pulled the trigger.

Mom had said my name. She's chosen to give me life over Quinn. I'd always justified my mother's actions, that there hadn't really been a choice. They would have kept hurting us.

Me and Quinn.

Not her.

Just like Artie'd said. He'd been adamant about that point. They'd never hurt Mom. She'd been made to watch at the end. She'd been in the room some of the time they were messing with us, but they'd never put a finger on her.

Even when they dragged her out of the room, and we thought they were doing horrible things to her, she always came back clean and untouched.

"Harley!" Zack calls to me, probably searching this massive place. But I'm exactly where he left me.

In this bed.

Wallowing.

She'd wanted me to die.

And then she pretended it wasn't so, that she hadn't made that choice. She acted like she mourned Quinn because she hadn't chosen her, but it was because she'd been tricked.

"Harley." Zack pushes the bedroom door open. "You're still in bed."

I roll over to face him.

"I like this bed. I may never leave it," I tell him and pull a pillow over my head.

A second later, it's yanked away, and his steely gaze pins me. "I brought food. Come eat."

"I don't want to eat." I try to grab the pillow back from him, but he tosses it across the room.

Why won't he just let me melt into the bed? I'm unwanted.

"If things had happened the way you thought you remembered them, and Quinn had survived, what would you tell her?" he demands. There's no softness here. He's all authority now.

I see the Marine in him with his set jaw, his battle stance.

Are we at war with each other, or the world?

"I have no idea." I lift my chin. "That Mom had to make a choice. But she didn't, did she Zack?" Shoving my elbows into the mattress, I push myself up and swing my legs around. He moves back just in time as I jump off the massive bed.

"We don't know the full story yet. And there's a chance that this memory isn't completely right, either. You're just starting to get more of them back. We don't know everything yet."

"We know my mother's not innocent. We know she's been pretending to be a loving, supportive mother for the last ten years, when in fact she was regretting that the wrong daughter lived." I stomp off to the attached bathroom and slam the door behind me.

He doesn't deserve my anger, but she's not here and I need

it to go somewhere. I need the pain rolling through my chest, stealing away my breath, to come out. It's going to suffocate me if it stays in.

The vanity in this insanely sized bathroom has six drawers. And not a single one of them has a razor, or a pair of scissors, or even nail clippers. Who doesn't have nail clippers?

I yank open the linen closet and find everything I need. Even a first aid kit to clean up after.

The bathroom door bursts open, banging off the wall and Zack's in here with me. Shoving the closet door closed and aiming his fierce gaze at the nail trimming kit in my hand.

"What do you think you're doing, little bird?" His chin is buried into his chest, and he's looking up at me through hooded eyes.

My breath catches as he taps a finger onto the plastic box in my hand.

"I need a minute," I tell him, some of the bravado slipping from my voice. He advances on me.

Step by step, he walks me across the bathroom until my back hits the wall. One hand slaps the wall to my left, another to the right. I'm neatly caged inside his storm.

I raise my chin, ready to take him on.

This isn't his pain to work through. It's mine. All mine.

"Are you afraid of me, little bird?" He levels me with his glare. Heat pools inside me when he stares at me with his darkness. "Are you afraid of what I will do to you?" He arches his left eyebrow, and it reminds me of the first time I saw him.

He's challenging me.

"No." I shake my head a little, my grasp loosens on the nail kit. "I'm afraid of what you won't do to me."

His other brow lifts. A smile tugs on his mouth until he's grinning like a proud papa.

"Give me the nail kit." He grips the box. "Let go, little bird, and I promise I'll make the outside hurt better than the inside."

I swallow back the sob threatening to break free. How can this man know me so well?

He sees the dark demons dancing, and instead of running away, he turns the music louder.

Closing my eyes, I release the box, and he takes it from me.

"Good little bird." He kisses my cheek. "Now, get rid of those clothes." He takes the box to the vanity and places it on the counter. He opens it up and looks at the tools inside.

My hands shake as I pull off the clothes I slept in and drop them into a pile beside the shower.

"Come here." He holds out his hand to me. In his other hand, he holds the pointed nail file.

His touch is warm when he wraps his hand around mine, leading me to stand in front of him.

"Up here." He pats the countertop, but before I can hop on, he grabs me by the hips and hoists me. The marble is cool against my ass.

"Zack," I whisper his name.

"Not yet, little bird. I'm playing." He pushes my knees apart and stands between them. "Now, your thighs are already pretty, let's work on your chest."

I dig my nails into my knees, readying myself for the bite.

"Eyes on me. Never look away." His orders are harder to obey now. Such fierceness shouldn't wet my pussy the way it does, but I can already feel myself dripping onto the counter.

"All right," I agree with a nod.

Placing the tip of the file just below my collar bone, where it won't be seen when I'm dressed, he pushes it into my skin.

At first, I don't feel much. It's not very sharp after all. But then he pushes harder, and harder still, until pain blossoms, spreading heat all throughout my chest, down my belly.

"Ahhhh." I fight the urge to pull back as he drags the file downward. Barely half an inch, but it's getting deeper, and the pain draws a fog in.

"Such a good girl." He lifts the file and brings the tip of it to his mouth. There's a tiny drop of blood, and he licks it away.

"More." I arch my back, offering him my body.

He grins like he's been given the keys to the kingdom.

The file digs in again, this time deeper right away. He's pushed through the skin, and I hiss from the instant burn. Blood trickles from the cut he's made, but he's not finished.

Carving my skin, he drags the tip across, then down and across again.

My toes curl.

The fog rolls in, thicker and sweeter.

"Is my girl happy yet?" he asks, wiping the trickle of blood off my skin with his middle finger and brings it into my eyesight.

"It feels good when you hurt me," I say, eyeing his bloody finger.

"I feel good when I hurt you, too." He brings the finger to my mouth, pushing past my lips, and I suck until the metallic taste goes away.

"More?" He poises the file over my chest again.

"Please." I nod and lean back, shaking my hair behind me to be sure his canvas is free of any obstruction.

He moves his eyes to my chest, leaving me to stare at the top of his head as he continues his work.

More carving, up, down. Over and then up, down, sideways.

I lose track of the direction of the file, as my chest fills with warmth. My body clenches, no longer in pain, but in want.

When he's finished, he brings his eyes up to mine. Light shines in the middle of the darkness.

"Do you want to see?" he asks, dropping the file to the countertop.

I nod, too aroused, too needy to open my mouth lest I'll beg him to fill me with something other than pain. And he's not finished playing.

I won't steal his joy from him.

He opens the top drawer in the vanity and pulls out a hand mirror. Aiming it at my chest, he angles it so that I can see the beauty he's created.

Z + H

He's carved our initials into my chest. Tiny pearls of blood bead up from the cuts in some areas. He catches a drop as it starts to roll down over my breast, and brings it to my mouth. This time he smears it across my lips, painting them as if it were lipstick instead of my own blood.

"You were so pretty with it before, I wanted to see it again," he admits, putting the mirror back in the drawer and dropping it. "How do you feel?"

I spread my legs more.

"I need you."

"I need you, too." He grabs at his belt, yanking at it until it opens and he's able to shove down his jeans and boxers. "I'm not going to be gentle, little bird. My cock's never been harder."

"No. Never gentle." I inch closer to the edge of the counter.

"I'm going to make it hurt," he promises, and my pussy weeps with joy.

"Please. Always." I suck in a breath when his hand sinks into my hair and he yanks my head back.

I can't see him. Only the ceiling as he thrusts his cock into me.

"Fuck you're wet." He bites down on my neck, twisting his hand in my hair until the burn in my scalp makes me whimper.

But he promised not to be gentle.

He vowed to make it hurt.

And he never lies to me.

His teeth drag across my collar bone, then up to my neck, where he bites into my shoulder.

"Zack!" I wrap my arms around him. "Oh, god!" I scream, pulling at him. And he doesn't disappoint.

He gives me everything I never understood I needed.

Wrapping an arm around my waist, he holds me steady while he plows into me relentlessly.

The edge of the counter digs into my ass, but it only drives me closer to the edge.

"Fuck," he groans, biting my earlobe.

"Oh! I can't...oh..." I throw my head back just as the storm crests and my body spirals with pain and pleasure. A dance so erotic, so sweet, it shoves me over the cliff, and I'm left panting and screaming his name as the waves of it all attempt to drown me.

"Fuck, Harley! Fuck!" He lets go of my hair, using both hands on my hips to pull me to him, driving full force into me again and again, until he stills. Unleashing his pleasure into me with a roar worthy of a warrior.

How fitting.

My warrior.

Moments later, he's carrying me back to bed. I've been washed and my cuts have been tended to. A small bandage covers our initials.

"I'm going to clean up in the bathroom. When I'm done, you need to be dressed so you can eat what I brought for you."

"You're being bossy, Zack," I say, leaning back against the pillows.

He touches the bandage covering our initials.

"You're mine now, little bird."

He walks back to the bathroom.

You're mine now.

I've never been so thrilled.

NINETEEN

Zack

Harley stands at the kitchen island with a greeting card in her hand.

She hands the card to me. "Who're Brian and Abigail?"

I read the thank you note quickly.

Thanks for the use of the place. Happy Hunting!
Love, Abigail and Brian.

"Friends." I put the card down.

"This place belongs to you? You own it?" She pushes a hip into the island as I walk away to the fridge and grab a bottle of water.

"I do." I take a long drink of the cool water, while my eyes devour the deliciousness of her in my kitchen. I don't use the place often. Chicago isn't my favorite city, but sometimes I need a place to let things cool where no one knows who I am, and I can blend into the craziness.

"This bunch of roses." She picks up the card again, and points to the black and red roses embossed on the top of the stationary card. "You have the same tattoo on your chest."

I swallow another gulp of crisp water.

"That's right. I do."

"What does it mean?" She eyes the handwriting on the card. Abigail wrote it, I can tell by the elegant script.

"It's the symbol for the group I work with." It's the easiest way to explain it. "Sort of like a hunting club." I half smile.

"I thought you said you were a Marine before."

I nod, screwing the cap on the bottle. She's been given a blow. Everything is going to come into question until she finds her solid footing again.

"That's right. I was. Now I work with a different sort of organization."

"Doing what? I mean, how can you afford a place like this?" She folds her arms over her stomach, propping up her breasts. A bandage covers my artwork. Our initials. Hers plus mine.

There's no question now.

She and I belong to each other.

"I told you what I do, Harley." I slide along the island until I'm right in front of her.

"How does that translate into a penthouse on Michigan Avenue?" She's getting more demanding in her questions.

I lift a finger to her jawline, tracing the tension there.

"Just because the military couldn't let me operate officially within their ranks, doesn't mean I completely walked away."

Her eyes widen. "Are you telling me that the Marines pay you to hunt down these monsters? And other people, too?"

"Not the Marines." I drop my hand from her cheek. "There's no official branch that covers this sort of thing. You won't find an item line on any budget for us."

She tilts her a little to the side. "You're kind of like one of those comic book heroes my dad loved so much, aren't you?" Her lips, full and pink, kick up to the side. "A dark caped crusader?"

I laugh, and it feels so fucking good. In my kitchen, with her, my mark fresh on her skin, a smile on her pretty lips.

"No, little bird. I don't think I'm anyone's hero."

"You're mine." She grabs my hand and squeezes. Hard. "You're the first person who wanted to get to the truth. Even the doctors always pushed for me to move on, to try and focus on the future, not the past."

I bring her hand to my mouth, kissing her knuckles.

"Are you feeling better?" She crashed hard after I put her to bed. When we'd arrived, she declined a tour and wanted only to get to bed.

"I was mean to you. I'm sorry for that." Her cheeks flush with the sweetest blush.

I shake my head. "You were perfectly you, Harley."

"I yelled at you."

"And it was hot."

"It was hot?" She laughs.

"Yeah, when you lose control like that? Fuck, it's hot. And it's even better because I get to be the one that reels you in." I touch the bandage on her chest. "That's what this means, little bird. You and me. Together."

With a featherlike touch, she fingers the edges of the bandage.

"Do you think it will scar?" When she lifts her eyes to mine, I see the hope there. She wants to wear my mark permanently.

Nothing would make me happier.

"I'm not sure. That nail file wasn't all that sharp, the cuts might not be deep enough to cause a scar. But I hope it does."

She tucks her bottom lip between her teeth, fighting a smile. She doesn't need to hide this part of her from me. It's what feeds me.

I pluck her lip out.

"If it doesn't scar, maybe you can do it again, but with your knife. That way it will." She reaches past me and grabs my bottle of water, takes a sip.

"Fuck, little bird," I groan, inhaling the sweet scent of my body wash on her skin. "You're perfect."

She laughs.

"I think my mother would disagree." She puts the cap back on the water and hops off the kitchen stool. "I mean, you don't choose the perfect daughter to be murdered."

"While you were napping, I did some more digging. Vince hangs at a bar called Cuffs, here in the city. About twenty-five minutes from here." I veer the topic to finding the clearly guilty, while the jury deliberates on the verdict of Nancy Turner.

"Do you think he'll know if my mom was involved or not?" The weight of her question pulls her lips down into a frown. "I don't think I can ask her about it. Not yet."

"I'm hoping he'll be able to shed light on a lot of questions we have." Not too quickly, though. He's earned himself a lot of punishment, and stringing out the interrogation would be more than welcome. "And no, you shouldn't ask your mom about it," I agree. "You shouldn't talk to her right now. In fact, no talking to anyone. You can't even call into work,"

"I'm not scheduled to work until Friday, but I don't want to just not show up."

"We have to assume that anyone you talk to is compromised. That agent isn't going to just let things lie, she's going to be looking for us. Which means she's going to be talking to your bosses, your co-workers, friends, landlord. Anyone that might know where you'd go, or if you've called them."

"Do you think she'll find Artie?"

"Not unless I want her to. He's fine where he is." No one will find him. It's one of the perks of working with my crew.

"Mom texted me; she wants to go for lunch tomorrow." She blows out a breath. "I know she tipped off Laurens, but maybe it was an accident? Mom wouldn't have told her if she thought it meant I was going to be hurt." Indecision cracks her voice.

"Did you answer her?" I should have taken her phone while she was asleep. Her location services are turned off, but a message or call might be enough for the Special Agent to get information about her whereabouts.

"No. I just left it. I didn't know what to say." Hurt still lingers in her expression. I can't imagine the betrayal she feels at the realization of what her mother did. Years of believing she was chosen to live, and because of that her sister had died, only to find out it wasn't true.

"When you're ready to talk with her, we'll see her." I wish my suspicions had been wrong. Harley deserves better. Quinn did, too. But the situation doesn't change because of wishes.

"So, you've lived in Chicago this whole time?" A change in topic is fine with me. The last thing I want is to see her pick at the wound her mother's actions have created.

"Not all the time. I have a few places across the country. Chicago isn't my favorite." I pick up a lock of her hair, roll it between my fingers. "At least it wasn't until now."

Her blush gets darker, and I wonder if I can make her entire body turn red with just my voice.

If not, I'm sure my toys will work.

Fuck. I want her again.

"I was thinking of coloring my hair." She takes the strands from my grasp. "Maybe red. I've always wanted to be a redhead."

I grin. "I think red would look good on you."

"If Agent Laurens is looking for us, it might be harder if I don't look the same, right?" She folds her hair in half and pulls it up. "Maybe I should cut it, too? Chop it at my chin?"

Turning her head one way then the other, she models the look for me.

"I like it longer." I pull it from her hands and wrap it around my fist several times then yank her to me. "If it's short, I can't do this." I yank her head backward and overtake her mouth.

Nothing has ever tasted as good as Harley's submission to my beast. Her hands rest on my shoulders when I deepen the kiss. She hooks one leg over my hip.

When I pull away, her lips are swollen, and her chest is heaving for breath.

"Get your shoes on. There's a stylist I've worked with before who can help with your hair if you really want."

"And the cut?"

"You're not cutting this hair." And that's that.

She smiles. "All right."

I slowly untangle my hand from her hair, and gently shove her in the direction of the door.

"Shoes." I slap her ass hard, propelling her a step.

As she walks through the swinging door, she throws me a smile.

I've never considered sharing my life with someone. Not after I chose this path. But Harley has changed all of that.

After I'm done taking out all of her monsters, I'm going to keep my little bird and keep her safe. If anyone tries to take her from me, I'm going to end them, too.

TWENTY

Harley

"What do you drink?" Zack asks me as he settles me into a booth.

"Uh, a whiskey sour." I haven't gotten a drink at a bar in ages, but I remember the sweet taste of it when I was in college.

Heavy music pumps through the speakers. It's a small dive bar, but it's packed with people in fetish wear. The black tank top and skirt I'm wearing helps me blend in enough that I'm comfortable, while Zack pushes his way through the crowd to the bar.

"Hey." A man in a black leather halter top stops at the table. "You come all alone?" he asks lifting his chin in my direction.

"No. He's getting me a drink." I gesture toward the bar.

"He shouldn't be leaving you all alone." He leans over the table, close enough for the stench of his beer breath to roll over me. "You look like a girl who needs looking after."

"I do?" I give a purposeful glance down at myself.

"Yeah. If you were mine, I wouldn't let you sit here by

yourself. I'd have you on my leash, at my side, at all times." He winks, then licks the top row of his yellowing teeth. Someone drinks way too much coffee.

"I think maybe you should go." I try to shoo him away like the annoying little fly he is, but he's stubborn and won't budge.

"See? You don't even have the right respect for a Top."

I laugh. "You aren't my Top. The only thing you are is a pain in my ass. Now, go before he comes back, and you make him angry."

He looks over his shoulder, probably checking if anyone's headed our way.

Zack doesn't work that way; he doesn't come when you're watching him. It's when you don't see him you should be worried.

But this asshole doesn't know that.

Yet.

"I think maybe you're lying about being here with someone." He leans even further into the booth. "And do you know what I do to naughty girls who lie?"

He lifts his hand, like he's going to touch me, but he stops just before his skin touches mine. His eyes, narrowed with fake dominance a moment ago, spread wide in pain. A soundless scream, and he's yanked back from me.

Zack stands there, our drinks safely on the table, and the wannabe Top lies on the floor cradling his hand.

"It's broken!" He finally finds his voice.

Zack drags him up to his feet and stares at the fingers bent in odd directions.

"Yep. They are." He lets go of him with a shove.

The crowd is large enough that we've gone unnoticed. So far.

"I tried to warn him." I reach over the table and pick up my drink.

"I'm sure he's learned his lesson." Zack picks up his beer.

"Fuck, Brad. Again?" Another man pops out of the crowd and stares at the bent fingers.

"This fucker broke my fingers," he shouts, but the music just swallows up the noise.

"Your friend here tried to touch what wasn't his," Zack says.

The other guy looks at me, then at Zack, and blanches. Zack's not dressed in any fetish clothing, just a black T-shirt and a pair of dark slacks. The tattoos on his forearms are all the information the man seems to need to make his decision. Best to leave us alone.

"Shit, they're really broken." He grabs Brad's wrist. "Let's get out of here. Sorry about him." He pushes Brad to get going, but Brad is hurting pretty bad and is starting to cry. It takes a while for his friend to get him to the front door.

"You think security is going to come over now?" I ask when Zack slides into the booth beside me.

"There's no security here." He lays his arm over the back of the booth, draping his hand over my shoulder. "I like this shirt."

I look down at myself and grin.

Our initials are displayed perfectly in the middle of the V-neck of the top. I have no doubt he knew exactly what he was doing when he chose the spot to display his artwork.

I sip my drink and watch people grinding on the makeshift dance floor.

"Do you see him?" I ask after I'm half done with my drink.

"Yeah. He's in the back there." Zack gestures with his chin. "He's talking with the owners of the club; I want to wait until he's alone."

"In this place? He'll never be alone."

"He'll leave through the back entrance. Probably best to grab him then, but I want to watch him first. See who he talks to, see if he does any other business here."

Zack knows more about this stuff than I do, so I don't

argue. I try to get a good look at Vince, but it's too crowded. I only see a glimpse of his face every now and then as people move around him.

I lean into Zack.

He runs his hand over my head, petting me.

"You look good as a redhead," he says in my ear. "Valerie was right not to go too red. This lighter shade is perfect."

"I always wanted to color my hair, but Mom wouldn't let me. She said women paid hundreds of dollars to get the blonde I had." Maybe she just wanted me to keep looking exactly like Quinn. I was a walking image of the daughter she'd chosen to keep.

"You still salty I wouldn't let Valerie cut it?" His chest rumbles with a chuckle.

"No." I fake a sigh. "I'll just let it grow out like Rapunzel."

He fists my hair, pulling my head back and glaring into my eyes. His eyebrow is arched in that way of his, challenging me to go toe-to-toe.

"I'm not salty." I grin. "But I do have to pee."

He unravels his hand from my hair, letting me start to slide out of the booth.

"Harley," he snaps my name, stilling me for a beat.

"It's all right. I'll be careful." I pat his arm. "I promise."

His jaw tenses. "Don't talk to anyone," he orders.

"Of course not." I give him a fake salute which makes his eyebrow arch to a steep point.

"If you're going to be bratty, I'm sure I can find someone here with a gag I can use." His voice is hard.

A memory flickers, but I easily shove it away.

Zack's not them.

"I've never been accused of being a brat before." I smile at him as I finish scooting out of the booth.

"No accusation. Pure facts." He leans back, hooking his arms over the back of the bench seat. "You have two minutes, little bird, before I come find you."

"I don't think that's the threat you think it is." I laugh. There's no point in ever thinking I could outrun him, but the chase would be exhilarating.

He shakes his head.

"Two minutes." He wiggles his fingers at me.

I head to the back of the bar toward the restrooms, working my way around the dancers and through the crowd at the bar. When I get closer to the restrooms, Vince comes into view. I don't recognize his face, but I can tell it's him, because everyone's sitting around him like he's some sort of god.

The bathroom is empty, so I'm able to get in and out quickly. If Zack says he's counting down the time, he's counting down the time.

I open the door to step back into the hall, but I freeze at a familiar voice.

"Well, I haven't heard back from him since yesterday." Agent Laurens.

I step back into the bathroom, shutting the door enough to shield me from her sight but still be able to hear her conversation.

"If he fucked up, he's probably hiding from you. I'm going out there tomorrow to pick up some product he's holding for me. I'll find out what's going on and get back to you."

Electric fear skims over my skin, setting all the little hairs on end.

That voice.

I have to clench my teeth together to keep from making a sound. It's Vince. It has to be.

"Fine. I expect to hear from you by tomorrow night." Laurens sounds shaky. Like she's losing control of her situation. "I've got Jimmy on me about Dustin going missing, and now his cousin is too. It's not good."

"What's that got to do with you?"

"I can only circumvent so many investigations at a time. Someone picks up on these guys having connections, and their bodies start showing up, it's going to be hard to get in front of it," Laurens says.

"Don't worry. Artie's just hiding from his fuck up, and Dustin probably took off on some bender. The younger girl, Jackie, is giving him a hell of a time. I'll pick her up and check in with you after I see him." Vince laughs. "Those motherfuckers. Always causing stress. Don't worry so much."

"Maybe you should worry a little," she bites back.

"Look. It's going to be fine. So what if the bitch remembers what happened to her? She can't prove anything, right? She has no idea where they were taken, and unless her mom decides to tell all of *her* dirty secrets, it won't matter."

"Her mom is another issue."

My heart stops.

"Why? If she does decide to get chatty, Jimmy'll take care of it."

"It's an issue because she's a beneficiary of the Plastics Pension fund."

I lean into the door just enough to see them. Laurens is tense, her fingers curl into her palms.

"Oh." Vince rubs his chin. "Well, if she's on his payroll now, then even better. Look, she was willing to put her fucking kid up for collateral in the first place, what's to say she'd give a shit now if we take out the other one?"

Laurens hooks her hands on her hips.

"Yeah. I guess you're right about that. I mean, this one isn't even the one she chose, right?" Laurens laughs.

My blood heats.

"Yeah, fucking Jimmy." Vince joins her in her enjoyment of my horror. "I got to get back to these fuckers. I'll check in with you tomorrow. Try not to worry so much."

"Yeah. Yeah. Tomorrow." She turns with him like she's going to follow him, but then stops. "I gotta piss before I go." She turns around on her heel and comes straight at the bathroom.

I let go of the door, jumping back from it. Before I can dive into a stall the door pushes open and she walks through.

Dropping my eyes to the floor, I walk forward, bumping into her shoulder.

"Shit. Sorry," I mumble and reach for the door.

"Hey. Wait." She stops just as I get my foot outside. Do I run? No. She's a cop, she'll chase.

Slowly, I turn, but don't look up.

"You dropped your phone." She hands me my phone that must have fallen out of the pocket of my skirt.

"Thanks." I snatch it from her and hurry out of the room, letting the door swing closed behind me.

I take in a deep breath as I hurry back to the booth where Zack is glaring at me.

"More than two minutes." He taps his watch.

I dive into the booth and slide up to him.

"Agent Laurens is here," I blurt out. "And Vince and her were talking in the hallway, so I couldn't get out of the bathroom. But then when they were done, she came in the bathroom."

I spill everything I heard them say.

"And when she came in, she picked up my phone and gave it to me. Zack, she looked right at me."

His attention snaps to the bathrooms. Agent Laurens is just stepping back into the bar. She keeps to the perimeter on the other side and goes straight for the exit.

"Did she not recognize me?" I grab his arm. "Is she just fucking with us?"

Zack wraps his hand calmly around mine, pulls it off his forearm, and brings it to his lips. He kisses the inside of my palm.

"She didn't recognize you because of your hair. You went from blonde to red, and she wasn't expecting to see you here. So, don't worry about her. It sounds like she has other worries at the moment."

I nod, take a deep breath, and sink back against the leather seat.

"Right." He's right. If she had recognized me, she wouldn't have let me leave the bathroom. "I'm glad I went with this color then."

"It's the perfect color for you," he says and kisses me. "Now, slower this time, tell me again what they said about the product."

I go over it again.

"I think he means people," I say. "I remember when...I remember Vince coming in one time. He said he was coming to sample the product." I squeeze my hand closed, digging my fingernails into my palms. "And he said a name. Jackie. So I think he's talking about people. Maybe more girls?"

Zack's features darken, and I see the beast in him slowly emerge. He downs the rest of his beer and snatches my hand, pulling me out of the booth with him.

"We need to get to them before he does."

TWENTY ONE

Zack

I look, but I find no traces of anything like what Harley described to me. No one connected to Arthur owns a warehouse or a workshop or mechanic's shop. Nothing that would have the oil and gasoline smells she remembers.

"I'm sorry I don't remember," Harley says quietly from the passenger seat in my car. We've been sitting in it for the past hour, waiting for Vince to come out to his own car.

It's midnight. The bar's open for another two hours, but he won't stay that long. Most of the assholes he was sitting with have already left.

"It's not your fault." I squeeze her knee, so she knows I mean it. "I'm sure Vince will be all too happy to show us the way." I cut my eyes to a figure walking toward us on the sidewalk.

His car, parked behind us, beeps, and the front lights flicker as he unlocks his Challenger. Other than him, the street is empty. He shouldn't have parked a full block away from the bar, but he's probably not expecting anyone to hold his ass accountable for any of the evil shit he's done.

"Wait here," I tell her as I open the middle console and pull out the syringe I prepped for tonight's clubbing adventure.

She gives a little nod, so I know she heard me, and she sinks lower in her seat to keep him from seeing her.

This man hurt her, and he's going to fucking pay a dear price for it. But first, we need information. So, he's not going to get his full punishment yet.

Steeling my anger, I quietly get out of the car as he approaches. He's got his head down, swiping through his phone while humming to himself.

Fuck, this asshole's oblivious.

I wait until he walks past my car before rushing him from behind.

His phone flies. I'll get it later. He screams from the surprise. The prick had no idea he wasn't alone on the street.

"What the fuck! Let me go!" His feet scramble for purchase as I wrap my arm around his neck, yanking him backward until he loses his footing and falls flat on his ass.

"I am going to fuck you up!" His empty threat dies in the midnight air as I sink the needle into his neck.

Wide, panicked eyes find mine, and he tries to hit my arm away. It's too late though, the drug's already in his system. Letting him go, I stand up and move back a step.

He thrashes, tries to get to his feet, to run away, but the drug is already working. Probably could have given him a higher dose; he shouldn't be this mobile right now, but that's fine, I can be patient when it's called for.

"What did...?" His eyes roll, and he folds, his knees hitting the sidewalk before he faceplants right into the cement.

There.

Harley pops the trunk open for me while I gather him off the sidewalk. He's bigger than Artie was, more muscle, and taller, too. With my arms hooked beneath his, I drag him to the back of my car.

"I can help." Harley hops out of her seat and grabs his booted feet. "He's big. Are you sure he'll fit?" she asks as we get to the trunk.

"Yeah, baby, he'll fit." I readjust my grasp. "On three, we're gonna lift and swing, yeah?"

"Got it." She gives me a firm nod and reworks her grab on his feet, so she's got a good grip on him.

"One...two...three!"

We hoist his ass up, then swing him into the trunk. His legs dangle out a bit, but that's fine. Humans are damn flexible when they're not awake to fight the pain of being stretched in a new way. I fold his legs in and contort him until he's stuffed inside.

Once I have his feet bound tight, and his hands tied behind him, I slam the trunk.

"I think you hit him with it." She winces.

I lift a shoulder. "That's nothing compared to what's coming to him." I gesture with a nod to the car. "Grab his phone and get in. It's late already."

She snatches his phone from where it flew off to, then jumps into her side of the car and buckles up.

"Are we going back to the storage unit?" She is almost giddy with the prospect of getting this monster off the streets.

I take his phone from her, cutting off the location services so he can't be tracked by his GPS.

I hand her the phone and shift into gear.

"There's a barn about forty-five minutes from here. That will do."

Vince is a heavy motherfucker, but we got him out of the trunk and onto the dolly so I could drag his ass into the barn.

"I think he's waking up." Harley hops off the surgical table and leans down to look up into his face. Slumped over the way he is, it's hard to get a good look at his eyes.

Fisting his hair in her hand, she yanks his head back and slaps his cheek.

"Yeah, he's getting there." She pushes his head back against the head rest. "Do you have some rope in here? We can just tie his head up."

"Good idea." I grab a leather belt from a drawer and bring it over to her. She uncurls the belt and straps it around his forehead and buckles it behind the chair. It's just small enough to hold his head up.

"There." She smiles at me, resting her hands on his shoulder. "Are his eyes open yet?"

"He's awake, but he's trying to keep his eyes closed." I curl my finger at her, beckoning her to my side. "This is how you know the difference between a man like him and a man like Artie. When Artie came to, he flopped around like fish pulled out of the water. Vince here is fully awake, but he's pretending to still be out so he can assess his situation."

"That's smart," she says.

"It's what I would do if I were in his position." The blade opening on my knife makes his muscles stiffen. Oh yes, he's very much awake. "Though if he doesn't open his eyes soon, I'm going to have to stick this knife into his kneecap."

Harley's lips curl with anticipation. She wants his blood.

She deserves his blood.

"Ah, there he is." She laughs when Vince's eyes pop open. He tries to move his mouth to speak, but the drugs are getting in the way.

"It'll be another minute before you can talk," I tell him, pressing the tip of my knife to his chin. "In the meantime, I'm going to ask you some yes or no questions and you're going to answer by blinking. One for no, two for yes. Understand?"

He stares up at me. His panic is well under control, and there's only a trace of fear on him.

Poor bastard still thinks he has a way out of here.

"The knife to the kneecap is still an option for noncooperation." I point the tip of my knife at his legs. "Do you understand what's happening?"

Two quick blinks.

"Good." I pat the flat of the blade against his cheek. "Do you work for Jimmy Blackwood?"

Again, his stare goes blank.

I sigh. This is going to be a very long conversation if he makes me hurt him every time I want an answer.

But he's a grown man, making his own decisions.

In a quick motion, I drive the knife just above his kneecap. A gurgling sound of a scream bursts from him, rising up in volume a bit toward the end.

Good, his vocal cords are starting to come back to life.

Jerking the knife back out, I bring the blood covered tip to his view.

"Do you work for Jimmy Blackwood?" I repeat my question.

Two quick blinks.

"See. All you have to do is answer."

"You move his product?"

Another two fast blinks.

"Great." I turn to Harley who's chewing on the inside of her lip. "He's finally getting the hang of this." She smiles a little, but having him so close to her has to be hard. This man hurt her. He played with her like she was some dirty toy for them to pass around.

"And product is girls?" I turn back to him, my skin hot.

"Y-yeah." He blinks but his mouth is working.

"Oh, good. You can talk." I step back a little. "You sell girls for Jimmy?"

He swallows then licks his dried-out lips. "I set up the sales, yeah."

"I thought Jimmy was in the loan sharking side of things. I'd heard Jacob doesn't like the flesh trade." And as big a deal Jimmy is in Chicago, his cousin, the head of the whole operation, is fucking huge in all major cities.

"He doesn't." He swallows again. "Jimmy takes the girls as payment." He coughs a little, turns his head best he can with the strap holding him in place, and spits on the ground.

"No fucking manners," I mutter. "What does that mean, payment?"

"If they can't pay, they put up collateral." His head rolls the side. The problem with this drug is, even when it starts to wear off, sometimes it kicks back in for certain muscles. If it wasn't for the strap, he'd be face deep in his chest again.

"So, if someone takes a loan from Jimmy, they have to put collateral in the form of a person?" Harley steps up.

His eyes roam over her. Memory strikes and all color drains from his face.

"Fuck," he moans.

"Fuck indeed," I laugh. "So, you realize now there's no happy ending here for you, right?"

He turns his gaze to me. "You took out Arthur?"

"Dustin too," I add.

"Fuck, man. It was years ago. And it was Jimmy."

"It was you, too." Harley straddles him in the chair, sitting on his lap. "You were there. You came in, you wanted to play. Don't you remember? You dragged me out of the room and put me in an office. You tied my hands behind my back, and you tied my ankles to the legs of the desk. You bent me over the desk, don't you remember?" She slaps him hard across the face.

"I wasn't wearing any clothes at that point; you'd already taken them from me." She slaps him harder, his head snaps.

"Don't you remember your little game?" She leans back, putting pressure on his wounded leg, making him cry out.

"I remember! Get off!" His bindings won't let him off the chair, and his muscles are too weak still to do much other than jerk.

"What was the game?" She scoots back more on his lap, and he howls. Blood soaks into his jeans, into her skirt.

"You might want to answer her, Vince." I hand her a knife, it's smaller than mine, and I was planning to give it to her later as a little present, but she's in need of it now.

"It was so fucking long ago," he wails.

She brings the knife up to his face. "What was the game, Vince?" She pushes the very tip of the knife against his neck until a small bead of blood forms.

"We don't want him dead yet, little bird," I remind her.

"I know how deep to cut before there's a problem," she says sweetly, pushing a tiny bit more.

He winces, finally sensing the danger.

"Hide the salami," he says with as much regret a grown man can show at such speaking such a juvenile phrase.

"That's right. You hid the salami, didn't you?" She drags the knife down his neck, cutting just deep enough to make him bleed, but not near any major arteries.

He hisses, tries to twist away from her, but she's in the zone.

She slices another bit and then another. Until his neck is drenched in his own blood.

When she's finished, she hops off his lap and stands next to me. Her hand drips his blood, and there's a small smattering of it on her cheek.

"I'm done playing now." She moves to hand me the knife back.

"It's yours."

"Good. I like it." She smiles and wipes the blade clean with her skirt. "Thanks."

"Just fucking kill me if you're gonna do it," Vince yells.

He's getting enough strength back that he actually got some bass behind his demand.

"Not yet." I drop my shoulders. "If you're really good and answer us, I won't make you suffer."

"Too much," Harley adds. "He needs to suffer some."

"Of course he does, little bird," I agree.

"Did my mother take money from Jimmy?" she questions.

"She was the one paid, but she didn't make the deal."

"Who did?" She steps closer, tension builds in her shoulders.

"Your father."

TWENTY TWO

Harley

"Dad?" Breathing is an impossibility for a moment. "Dad sold us to Jimmy?"

Vince shakes his head against the belt.

"No. He sold your mother. I don't know all the details. Only that he took the loan 'cause he was so sick, and he knew there wasn't anything after he died. So, he took the loan, put your mom up for collateral if he couldn't find a way to get a life insurance policy to cover him."

"Of course they wouldn't. He was dying of cancer." The knife in my hand becomes a lifeline, ready to plunge into him.

"Then how did her sister and her get caught up?" Zack questions.

"I don't know. I only know I was to get the three of them and put them up for auction."

"But Jimmy is the one that came that last night." At least it seemed like night. When the garage door opened that last time, no sunlight poured in. It had to be night.

"I don't know." His gaze flickers between me and Zack, like he's trying to find out if there's any hope left of him surviving this visit. "Jimmy makes the rules, I just do what I'm told. Arthur holds the product until it's ready to move. That's his job."

"And Dustin?" Zack asks.

"Dustin was Arthur's bitch; he does what Artie tells him to." He winces as he tries to move against the binds.

"Special Agent Laurens works for Jimmy then, too?" Zack continues his questions. I move back to the metal surgical table and hop on top.

The knife Zack gave me clanks against the metal.

Dad sold Mom.

They were happy together. Mom loved him. Losing him had been soul crushing. I witnessed it. Even though he'd been so sick, and death was a reprieve when it finally came calling, she had held onto hope that some miracle would save him. She would have given up everything to save him, to have just a little more time with him.

Why would he do such a thing?

He was going to leave us with no mother?

"The pension Mom just started getting." I cut off whatever Zack is saying to him. "She's getting that because of something with Jimmy. What is it? Blackwood." I look to Zack. "She has a section in her binder, the one with all Dad's paperwork has a tab labeled Blackwood."

Zack takes a small step to the left so I can see Vince from where I'm sitting.

"Some pension scam. Laurens said she's a beneficiary, so she's probably cleaning money for him." He looks to Zack. "Look, I'm telling you the truth here. I'm giving you what you want. So just let me go."

"Let you go?" Zack laughs. "You've admitted to selling girls to the highest bidder to be taken away by fucking monsters to have their way with them. You admitted to raping my girl. You admitted to helping Jimmy kill her sister. You've given me a lot of information. So, I won't start cutting off body parts, but you're not getting out of this fucking place alive."

"Jimmy killed that girl. Not me. Jimmy. I don't fucking kill people."

Jumping off the table, I rush him with my knife back in my hand.

"You don't fucking kill people?" I plunge the blade into his shoulder, then his arm, then his side before Zack yanks me off.

"Shhh, little bird. Not yet." He spins me to face him and wipes my face. I've started crying sometime after Vince's last stupid statement.

"He's lying," I whisper. "He killed me a little when he did those things. He killed Quinn when he did the same to her. He killed my family."

Zack nods. "He did, I know. He's going to pay." It's a promise. He doesn't lie. Closing my eyes, I take a breath, then another, until the rage quiets in my mind and Vince's whimpering comes through.

"Man, she's crazy!" he yells.

Zack's features darken. A quiet falls over him. "Crazy?" He turns to him, leaving me and walking over to him. "You sell girls, and you think she's crazy for wanting you dead?"

Vince blanches. "I didn't mean to insult your girl."

"Insult her?" Zack laughs, but there's no joy. Vince has opened the gate and Zack's beast is coming out. "Of all the things you've done to her, you think an insult is going to be the thing that gets you killed?"

"I'm trying to help you out!" He's panicking now, wiggling more and more, trying to get out of the ropes. But Zack ties a good a knot. There will be no escape.

"We need one more thing from you." I move to stand behind him. "You said you're picking up product tomorrow." I put my hands on his shoulders. The tip of my knife brushes against the open wounds on his neck.

"Where?" Zack asks.

"You want to know that, you gotta promise to let me go," Vince tries to bargain. A horrible move on his part. Zack doesn't make deals with monsters.

"You are a stubborn prick, you know that?" Zack gives an empty laugh. "Here's the deal. You like buying and selling things, right? You make your money doing that. So, here's what we're going to do." He turns and points at the digital camera he set up that's aimed at us.

"What the fuck is that?" Vince whispers.

"Nothing yet. But I'm gonna turn it on and then we're going to take orders." He points to the laptop sitting on a folding table next to the camera. "And when there's an order for your toe, I'll cut off your toe. When there's an order for your thumb, I'll take the thumb. Are you getting what I'm saying here, Vince?"

Vince's chest heaves. "You're sick," he whines.

"Sick of you? Yes. Sick of the monsters in this world? Fuck yes." Zack moves to the computer and turns it around so we can see the screen. "Just need to open the store. Looks like there's already about fifty fuckers in queue to sign in."

"Now." I squeeze his shoulders. "Where's the *product*, Vince?"

TWENTY THREE

"Girls?" Mom's hoarse voice wakes me from what light sleep I've been able to find.

Rolling my head back, I try to focus on her. It's been dark for so long now; I can see pretty well through it.

"Yeah, Mom?" My sister's voice is getting weaker. She's getting weaker as the time passes. I reach over to her, sliding my hand through the dirt and grime covering the cement floor. When our fingers touch, she flinches.

"It's just me." I cover her hand, squeezing it. She's taken so much more of the abuse. They consider her the pretty one.

Between the two of us, everyone's always thought she was the prettiest, and I've always thought it was my curse.

"I don't think they're coming back," Mom says. "We should try to get to get these chains off again."

"I'm tired," my sister whispers. "I'm so tired."

"I know, sweetie, but we have to get to the door," Mom directs us. "Maybe if we all grab hold of one chain, we can break it?"

"We tried that already," I point out. Mom's tried to keep us talking, to keep us aware, but it seems her mind has started to slip.

Going this long without any light. Not knowing what time or what day it is. It's bound to mess with our minds.

"It's been days, I think," I say, squeezing my sister's hand again. "But we'll be okay. They'll come in and give us water." I'm not so sure about that anymore, though. They've never gone this long without bringing us at least a peanut butter sandwich, and a bottle of water.

"We're no good to them dead." My sister repeats my words back to me, and tightens her grip around my hand.

She's gotten so weak.

"How is your side?" I lean toward her, trying to feel down her ribcage, but she's too far away. We're only able to touch hands when we stretch the chains out to the max.

"It's fine. I promise." She laughs. "I've been meaning to lose a few pounds anyway." The little joke gives me hope she's not too far gone. They haven't beaten her soul.

"I'm so sorry, girls." Mom's sob breaks her sentence. "I don't understand why this happened. I don't understand."

"It's all right, Mom." I let go of Jackie and scoot over to my mom, reaching as far as I can until I can touch her. "It's not your fault."

"It is." She pulls her hand away. "It's my fault. I can't believe this happened."

My spine stiffens. We've been locked in this awful place forever, and she's never spoken about this. "Do you know these guys?"

"No." Her sniffle breaks through the darkness. "But one of the names, Jimmy. I heard of him. Steve did this."

"Steve?" Her current boyfriend. "How did Steve do this?"

"He's always losing money, borrowing money, and he took money from some guy– Jimmy. Steve said he had to put up a lot of collateral for the loan, but not to worry. He'd pay it back." Another sob. "I think it was us. I think we're the collateral."

"Steve told these guys to hurt us?" Jackie's voice gets a little stronger.

"I think he let them." Mom yanks on her chains. "If I can just get my foot out. I can get to the door. I can get us out. I can save us." She's hysterical now. Metal scrapes along the concrete. The chains jangle as she fights with her bonds.

"Mom. Mom. Mom!" My throat aches when I yell. "Stop. You're just going to make your ankle bleed again. There is no getting out of these chains."

She continues to struggle with them.

"Just let her." Jackie's voice is a whisper now. "I need to close my eyes for a few minutes."

"No. Jackie, stay awake. We'll sleep in a little while. Mom's going to calm down. We're going to find a way out. And then we're going to find fucking Steve." There. We just need goals. And finding Steve is mine.

"Just a few minutes, Charlie. Just a few minutes." Jackie's chains jingle as she repositions herself, lying down with her head away from me. I can't reach her now, she's too far.

"No. Don't fall asleep yet. Mom's going to calm down. We're going to get out of these fucking chains." My fingers curl into my palms, digging my nails into my skin. "We are getting the fuck out of here!" I scream into the darkness.

I'm tired too.

Bone tired.

But we can't sleep.

We might not wake up.

I scream again. I don't scream for help, because no help is coming. I don't scream anyone's name, because they won't hear me. I just scream.

A wretched sound that stretches my throat until I can almost feel it splitting.

And when I'm done, and my throat burns like I've swallowed a lit match, and my chest heaves searching for air, I lean my head back against the wall.

"Please," I whisper into the blackness of the room. "Please don't let us die like this. Not like this."

Mom sniffles.

Jackie makes no sound.

A bang draws my attention. Metal being hit with something hard, like a hammer.

No, bigger.

Another bang.

I squint my eyes toward the door. No one's there.

It gets louder.

And louder.

Until the door flies open and light, bright as the sun itself, floods the area, blinding me when I look toward it.

Oh, no. They're back.

Jackie's asleep. She won't be able to fight them. She's too tired.

Mom's crying gets more intense. She must see them too.

"Oh, god! There they are!"

TWENTY FOUR

Harley

It's pitch black in here, but there's enough light from the hallway that I can see three figures lying on the floor.

Gasoline and oil smells fill my nostrils, dragging up memories I don't have time for. Fighting back the flashes of figures walking through shadows, echoes of screams long past faded into the darkness, everything in me clenches.

This place is a war zone. Demons and monsters clash, and only the strongest will survive.

Proudly, my demons walk with me as I move toward the three figures folded into themselves on the cold, concrete floor.

"It's gonna be bright as hell. Cover your eyes," Zack announces just before he flips the lights on.

"Shit." The girl in the middle puts her hands over her eyes. "Too bright."

"Can you turn them down?" I look to the switch. There's no dimmer. Of course not, it's a mechanic's shop. There's on or off.

"Sorry. No." Zack frowns, then turns his attention to the

three women. The one on my left is asleep, the one to the right is a tearful mess.

"Oh god." I run to the sleeping one. "Is she all right?"

"Who are you?" the girl in the middle demands. "Don't touch her!" she screams at me when I reach for the sleeping figure.

"See. I told you I heard screaming," I say to Zack.

"Don't touch her!" Chains rattle as she lunges at me.

"It's all right." I back off from the sleeping figure. "We're going to get you out of here," I say. Zack helps me get back to my feet and pulls me away from the girls.

"They're scared, let's give them a second," he reassures me. "They don't know who we are."

I nod, looking them over as terror bubbles up in my stomach.

"This is the place, Zack." My whisper is hoarse. "I was there." I point to the middle girl. "Quinn was there." The sleeping girl. "And Mom, when they had here in here, was there." I point to the oldest of the three women.

"You're not there anymore, little bird," he reminds me. He's so patient with me.

"You were here?" the girl in the middle asks, dropping her hand from her eyes and blinking against the light. They've been darkness for days, maybe longer. It's going to take a while before their eyes adapt to any light.

"I was. Right where you are." I nod. "I know you're really scared right now, but we are here to help you. The others aren't coming back." I step toward her. "They are *never* going to hurt you, or anyone, again."

Dirt clings to her blonde hair. It's matted and tangled all around her head. Black smudges cover her cheeks. Dried blood is everywhere; on what's left of a nightgown, her arms, her chin, her thighs.

I groan when I see the dark brown spots on her thighs. How many times did she have to endure their touches? My insides clench so hard at the anger boiling up, I'm afraid I'm going to vomit.

"He hurt you so badly," I whisper squatting at her side. "Don't worry, I hurt him even worse." I hope I did these women justice.

"You hurt him?" she asks moving her gaze to Zack who is digging through tool benches.

"The first thing we cut off of him was his dick," I assure her with a smile.

Her lips spread into a grin. The white teeth are a stark contrast to her dirty face.

"Which one was he? The big one?"

I nod. "Vince. Yeah. Artie's gone too; he can't touch you again." I pick up the thick chain links. They're heavier than I remember. My ankles had bruises from the shackles for weeks. The same marks are on her.

I touch the purple splotches. "We'll get these off. I promise."

"Thank god you're here," the older woman finally speaks, wiping her dirty hands across her face. She's as filthy as the other girls.

"Are you their mom?" My tone flattens. History repeats itself.

"She is, and she's not doing good. She keeps talking gibberish and then she's reasonable. I think we were left in the dark too long." The girl points to the sleeping figure. "That's Jackie, she's my sister. They hurt her the worse. I tried to keep her awake, but she keeps sleeping."

"Jackie. Got it, and you?"

"Charlie." She sits up a little more, wincing with the movement. "That's our mom, Sharon."

"I'm Harley." I try to smile. "I'm going to check on Jackie, all right?" She needs to feel comfortable with us. It's going to be hard for her to trust anyone after what they've endured. I won't do anything that she doesn't give the okay to. It's obvious, between the three of them, she's been carrying the strength. Without her, they would have collapsed into their terror much sooner.

"Yeah." She nods. "I think her ribs are broken, be careful."

"Okay." I crawl over to the sleeping girl. She's completely naked, covered in bruises from top to bottom. I brush her hair from her face and her eyes slowly blink open. "There you are." I smile softly. "We're not going to hurt you."

She licks at her dried, cracked lips and gives a tiny nod.

"I'm so tired." Her voice barely registers, it's so soft.

"It's all right. You rest. I'm going to find some water while Zack, that's my boyfriend over there, he's going to cut these chains off, all right?" I gently move her arm away from her torso, and see the dark purple bruise over her ribs. When I touch her, she jumps. "Shit, sorry. Sorry. I won't touch that again. I think your sister's right, they're broken."

"Me too." Jackie winces. "They kicked me so many times when I wouldn't–" Tears roll down her face, leaving clean streaks among the grime and dirt of her cheeks. "So then I did. I let them–"

"Not your fault," I say firmly, just like Zack did for me. "Nothing in this place was your fault. You survived. That was your job. And you did it. You survived." I'm not sure who I'm talking to more here, these women or myself.

She licks at her cracked lips some more and nods.

"I'm gonna find water. Zack's got the bolt cutters. Just do what he says, okay? He's a little scary looking but he's a good guy," I assure them. "He's the best."

"All right." Jackie nods again, and slowly shoves herself up to lean back against the wall.

"There's what looks like a break room over there. Maybe there's a sink." Zack gestures to a door in the corner of the room as he kneels down by the naked girl.

I freeze every time a chain drops onto the floor. Trying to distract myself, I focus on grabbing the water bottles from the mini-fridge in the break room. Leftover burger wrappers litter one of the tables, and the trashcan is full of beer cans. These assholes were here, watching these girls in their hell from the window of the room, while having burgers and beers.

The urge to kill them again overwhelms me.

Another chain clanks to the concrete, and I freeze.

Deep breath in.

Slowly let it out.

I'm free of this place.

And now they are, too.

Zack has them freed by the time I get back, and I hand each of them a bottle of water.

"Thank you." Charlie opens the bottle and starts gulping it down.

"Slow," I tell her. "Or you'll throw up." She stops drinking and nods.

Jackie can't hold the bottle long, so she takes small sips then puts it down. She's so pale beneath all the dirt on her face.

"I have people coming." Zack brings blankets from wherever he found them, and hands one to each of them. "They're going to take you to the hospital."

Charlie takes the blanket and scoots over to her sister, wrapping one around her naked body.

"See, Jackie, you're gonna be fine. We're going home." Charlie hugs her.

Sharon pushes herself up to her feet and staggers over to her daughters. Tears roll off her cheeks.

"I'm so sorry, girls." She sits between them, pulling them to her.

"Did you do this?" I accuse her with a hard tone that I can't hide.

Sharon turns her exhausted eyes up to me. "What?"

"Did you sell your girls to these people?"

"No." She shakes her head. "The man I've been seeing...I

think it was him. I'm positive it was him." Her expression hardens. "He can't get away with this."

"He won't," Charlie promises. "Who is coming? Your boyfriend said he has people coming?" Charlie asks me.

"I have two men coming, Jax and Casper." Zack squats down by the huddled women. "They are going to take you to the hospital, and they'll stay there until you feel safe. If you tell them to leave, they will. If you ask them to stay, they will. Their job is to protect you until you're ready to be without them. For however long that takes."

"You said they're all dead, though." Charlie turns her eyes to me.

"They are. But that doesn't mean you're done being scared." I frown. The fear lingers. It stains your soul if you try to ignore it. When you shove the demons beneath the bed, they'll haunt your dreams. It's better to let them into bed with you. Let them keep you safe.

She nods. "They'll stay with us when we go home?"

"They don't have to stay with you inside, but they'll keep watch on the house, on you girls," Zack explains. "You're the boss. You tell them what you need. It's their job to do it."

"And what about Steven?" Charlie's voice hardens. It's easy to see the strength in her. She's kept them strong during this nightmare.

Zack looks up at me over his shoulder.

"When you're ready, if you decide you want to deal with him, Casper will tell you how to get in touch with us," Zack says.

"Are you not staying now?" Jackie asks when Zack gets back to his feet.

"There's one more monster to deal with," he tells her.

The door opens behind us and the girls gasp, huddling together even tighter.

"Hey guys." Zack walks off to greet his friends. They're all just as tall and big as him. And dangerous looking.

"This is Casper," Zack introduces the bald one. He wears the same cluster of black and red roses on his forearm.

"That one is Jax." Zack points to the dark haired one. His tattoo is on his neck, right over his Adam's apple.

If I didn't know they were the good guys, I would be frightened.

"You're not the police then." Charlie tightens the blanket around her shoulders as she stands next to me.

"No. We're not the police. But, if you want them, we can call them," Casper offers.

"No." The word is given hard, without hesitation. "They'll get in the way."

I wrap one arm around her shoulders.

"You did good, Charlie. You kept them as safe as you could." She needs to hear it, and when her body softens, I know I was right.

"I wish I'd been there when you cut off his dick," she says.

"He cried like a baby," I promise her.

"I hate him. I hate all of them." The venom in her voice is enough to kill, I think.

I squeeze her a little. "Hate them for as long as you need to. But don't forget to let some love in later, when you're done hating. Love for yourself. For your mom and sister."

"Mom's boyfriend did this," she says with disgust. "We're sure of it."

"Like Zack said, when you're ready, you'll get in touch with us." I pat her shoulder. "Will you be okay with these guys?"

"Charlie?" Casper steps up to us. His eyebrows are up high, like he's trying to gauge her reaction to him, and his voice is soft. "We're going to take it from here, if that's all right with you. It looks like your sister needs medical attention right away. We can go to a hospital, or I have private doctors that can help. It's up to you where we go. Either way, me and Jax are with you as long as you need us."

She slides her gaze to me.

"Zack wouldn't let them near you if they weren't good guys," I assure her.

"All right then," she whispers, but there are tears in her eyes. "The hospital will have to call the police, won't they?"

"Sometimes they will, sometimes they won't. But with the three of you showing up with these types of injuries, my guess is they'll want to," Casper explains patiently. "But again, if you don't want to talk to the police, you don't have to, even if they get called."

"It's okay. You can go to the hospital if you want. You have no reason to trust any of us, but I promise you're safe now." My words are just that, words. It's going to take more than just a promise from me that she's safe before she'll be able to believe it. Trust will take even longer.

"The hospital is fine. If we want to leave, they'll let us, right?"

Casper nods. "I won't let them keep you against your will." He reminds me of Zack, the way his promise sounds so concrete. He won't let anyone hurt them.

"What should we do?" she asks her mom.

"I think you're right, let's go to the hospital." Sharon nods.

It's going to make things a little more difficult for them, because they'll have to answer a lot of questions. But they have every reason not to want to go anywhere private with these guys. Hell, even leaving here with them is risky.

"All right. We're gonna get you comfortable, then take you by ambulance to the hospital." As he speaks, Jax wheels in a gurney for Jackie. She's the most injured.

"Harley, we've got to go. Let the guys do their thing," Zack whispers in my ear, tugging on my arm.

"Yeah. Okay." I hug Charlie then look over at her sister and her mom. They're leaning against each other. Sharon is holding her daughter in her arms, stroking her hair. "Okay."

"These guys can get a hold of us right away, if you need something. All right?" I squeeze her hands.

Tears well up in her eyes.

"It's all right, Charlie. It's over." But not really. It won't be, until every image of what's happened to her, to her family, has been processed and she can beat them down again. The physical part is done, but the rest of her journey is just beginning.

"Okay." She flicks away a tear as Casper brings another gurney over to her. "Thank you. Thank you so much for finding us."

Casper easily picks her up and lays her on the bed, immediately covering her with her blanket and getting her comfortable.

"They're going to be okay, little bird," Zack assures me as he opens the passenger door of his car for me.

"Maybe we should let them come when we talk with Jimmy." I watch through the window as Casper eases Charlie into the back of an ambulance. Jackie's next in line.

Zack gets behind the wheel.

"They're not ready for that yet. They need to heal a bit first. Don't worry. Charlie reminds me of you. She'll get in touch when she's ready. Then she can really heal." He puts the car in gear and tears out of the parking lot behind the mechanic's shop.

We're fifty miles outside the city in a tiny-ass town. Not a single house or business for fifteen miles in either direction.

Even if we'd been able to get out of the shop, we'd have been too lost to figure out how to get home.

"Jimmy's next, right?" I watch the shop fade into the side-view mirror.

"Tonight, little bird. We check in on him tonight."

TWENTY FIVE

Zack

"If you go after him, you know his cousin has to retaliate." Jeff, the voice of reason.

"I have no fight with Jacob. If he wants to try and find me later, he's welcome to. I've gotten pretty good at hiding." Leaning back in the recliner, I stretch out my legs. The last few days have been intense. And once Jeff stops trying to play mother hen and gives me the information I need, tonight's going to be just as bad.

"Okay, you've been warned."

"You think he should get a pass because he's related to some big mob boss?" It's an accusation, but Jeff's never tried warning me off a kill before.

"Fuck no." He lets out a heavy sigh. "You already have to keep the locals off your back. Even with the help we all give, it's hard. To add the fucking Mafia to that, it could make your job harder."

Haugh.

"You'd feel better if I asked Jacob's permission first? Isn't that how they do things? Go up their chain and get Daddy to say yes first?" I've probably watched too many movies.

"Would you do that?"

"Fuck no." No laughter now. "I don't ask permission."

"Okay. Okay." There's tapping on the other end of the line. "I have it." Another sigh. "It's nasty, Zack. The shit that's in this club. It's horrific."

"It's a hardcore BDSM club, right?" I've been to plenty of those in my time. My line of work doesn't really give me time for date nights. A trip to a local club where I can find someone who wants exactly what I can offer has always served me well.

"No, not really. In those clubs, consent means something. Not here."

"Is it pay to play?" I pinch the bridge of my nose. Monsters lurk everywhere, and the more I take out, the more I find.

"Yeah. But you can bring your own girl, they don't make you purchase one or anything like that. I'm going to send you the location and the passcodes for tonight. It changes twice a night. These codes will work after eight."

"Any sort of security I need to be worried about?"

"Just the usual bouncer types. The four-digit code gets you into the building, the six-digit code gets you in the elevator. Once you're in there, you're fine."

"Really? It's that easy?"

"These people are comfortable in their depravity, Zack. They have everyone in their pockets—police, politicians, local and federal. They think they're bullet proof."

I grunt.

"Not from me."

"That's true." He laughs.

"How'd you get these codes if they change so often?"

There's a long pause.

"Jeff." I push the recliner forward, dropping my feet to the floor. "What."

"We've been watching this place for a while. Like I said,

it's nasty shit in there." Another pause. "Try to control the urge to take out everyone you see, yes? Deal with your guy. Later, the club will be dealt with."

"I make no promises, but I'll do my best." A clanking from the kitchen draws my attention. Harley's been in there a while, making lunch. "If anyone touches her, though—"

"That goes without saying." He cuts me off. "I'll get those codes sent over within the hour. I'm also going to send you the contact information on Jacob Blackwood. Just in case you decide to reach out."

"Thanks." I end the call on my way to the kitchen, freezing at the swinging door when I hear a sniffle.

"What's wrong?" The door swings back at me once I'm inside, searching for her.

Harley stands at the stove, sucking on her finger.

"I burnt it," she explains with it still in her mouth.

"Put it under cold water." I grab her wrist and pull her to the sink, throwing on the cold water tap and running her finger under it. It's red, but it won't blister.

While the water does its work, I run my thumb over her cheek, collecting the last tear rolling down.

"Your tears are so sweet," I say, licking it from my thumb.

She smiles.

"You said the same thing about my blood."

"It's true. Everything about you is sweet." I turn the tap off and take a closer look at the burn. "You'll live."

She laughs, and it's such a freeing sound. It's been so long since a pretty noise like this eased me. But it's not just her laugh, or her smile. It's everything about her.

She touches me and my body tingles. A simple look from her, and my cock gets hard. Just being in the same room with her makes my nerves calm. I breathe better with her around.

"I was making grilled cheese. You want one?" She hurries to the stove and moves the frying pan off the heat. "Good. It didn't burn."

"I'm hungry." I put my hands on her hips, nuzzling into her neck. "But not for grilled cheese."

"I can make you something else, if you want." She turns around in my grasp. "Oh." Her bottom lip disappears between her teeth when she catches my gaze.

"Yeah. Oh." I pick her up, tucking her legs around my waist, and carry her to the table.

I lay her across the table, not giving a fuck about the floral arrangement that falls to the floor with a clatter.

"I think it broke." She tries to check on the pottery pieces strewn on the floor.

"Don't care." Her jean shorts have a row of buttons instead of a zipper. The style should be outlawed. It takes way too long to get them all undone. Once the torture of the buttons is over, I rip her shorts and panties off, tossing them over my shoulder.

She giggles when I pull up a chair and sit down at the table.

"What are you doing?" She tries to sit up, but one arch of my eyebrow and she lies back down.

"I told you, I am hungry." Hooking my arms beneath her, I drag her ass to the edge, putting her pretty pussy right in front of me.

The moment my tongue touches her clit, she hisses, and it's an even prettier sound than her laugh. Biting down on the sensitive bud gifts me with another sound, and a wiggle.

She tastes of heaven coated in chocolate. Her moans mingle with mine as I devour what's mine. Sinking two fingers into her tight passage has her arching up at me. Sucking her clit into my mouth, I flick my tongue across it, while twisting and turning my fingers inside of her.

"Zack." She fists my hair, pulling.

"Fuck yes, baby, come for me. Give me all your juices." I bite down on the inside of her thigh, then go back to licking and sucking and biting every part of her until her body tightens. A tremble works through her thighs, and I thrust my fingers harder, adding a third, and curl them just enough to bring her the very edge.

"Fuck!" she screams as her body folds and her pussy squeezes my fingers. She floods my fingers with her release, and I catch every drop of her pleasure on my tongue. Licking her tenderly, and slowly, until her body eases back onto the table and she's fisting her own hair, catching her breath.

"Such a good girl," I wipe the back of my hand across my mouth, then shove the chair out of the way as I stand.

She looks down the length of her body at me, a sated grin on her lips.

"You didn't think I was that generous, did you?" I shove my pants down, fisting my cock. Just a little squeeze. Enough to take the edge off my arousal.

"We'll break the table," she warns.

I push the head of cock against her entrance.

"Fuck the table." In one powerful thrust, I'm inside her and the entire world stills.

This.

Right here, being inside her. Having her. Being with her.

It's all I need.

Evil quiets.

And for this moment, there's nothing but love.

Gritting my teeth, I drag her closer to me, thrusting harder and harder into her hot, wet pussy. Her ass slaps my thighs as I fuck her, growling at the pleasure of chasing down my release.

She reaches up, touching my face.

"Harder. Please. Harder."

"Fuck." I withdraw from her and grab her by the hair. She yelps, but there's a smile on her lips, and her pupils explode with arousal as I yank her from the table and flip her around.

"Ass out, baby." I slap her ass as she leans over the table. She pushes her ass up at me, offering herself. The red mark from my hand makes me crave more. I smack her again and again until her cheeks practically glow.

"Fuck yes," she moans.

Spreading her asscheeks, I push my cock into her pussy. She sucks up every inch. I can barely breathe it's so beautiful.

Another smack, and I'm fucking her again. The table scrapes against the tiles with each thrust.

Over and over again I spank her, I fuck her, and I crave her.

"Mine!" I yell just as I sink once more into her and my own release steals me away.

"Zack." Her sweet voice brings me out of the fog I'm lost in.

"Shit. You okay?" She's pressed into the edge of the table with me lying on top of her.

"I'm fine. But you're getting a little heavy," she laughs.

I pull out from her body, immediately missing her as I right my clothes.

"Can you get me a towel?" she asks as she stands upright. My cum drips down the inside of her left thigh.

"No." I kiss her forehead. "I like it on you like that." I gather up her shorts and panties, bringing them to her.

"I do too." She grins while stepping into her shorts.

I look over at the grilled cheese in the pan.

"Eat your lunch, then take a nap. We're going to have a late night tonight. You'll need your rest." I'll explain about the club later. She needs a good rest, and she won't get one if she's worrying about later.

"Will you nap with me?" She tucks her chin. The woman is as unstable as I am.

"Of course." I wink.

She's fucking perfect.

TWENTY SIX

Zack

"Holy shit." My mouth waters the second my eyes feast on Harley.

A sweet pink hue touches her cheeks, and she lowers her gaze.

"It's all right then?" She brushes her hand over her hip.

The deep-red slip dress she's wearing hugs her body in a way that makes my hands jealous. It hits mid-thigh, showing off her delicious legs. Her scars peek out, but they're part of her beauty. Every one of them helped saved her from drowning in the darkness.

"It's perfect." I pull her into me, running my fingertips along the deep neckline that dips between her breasts and tracing our initials. The thin scab has fallen off, leaving a raised pink outline of our letters. It may scar just enough for us to see it.

"I'm going to have to kill a few men tonight, I think." I kiss her cheek. At the very least blind the fuckers.

Her lips twist into a worried frown.

"What's wrong, little bird?" I ask, kissing the edge of her mouth.

"Have you ever hurt someone who didn't deserve it?" Her warm brown eyes align with mine, and there's the tiniest of wrinkles between her brows. I wonder how long she's been thinking to ask me this.

"No," I answer firmly. "And I never will." It's a vow I made to myself a long time ago.

She relaxes in my arms. "These other men you work with, Casper, Jax, and Sam, how do you know them?"

"We met after being stationed in the same shithole. Friends of friends, you might say. I trust them, and everyone I work with." Directly or indirectly. Our network is small, but it's powerful. All of us chase the monsters that created the demons inside of us.

"So, you don't work for bad people?"

I let her go and step back. "No, little bird. I don't work for bad people."

I grab my wallet that's sitting on the end table and tuck it into the back pocket of my slacks. After looking around, I find my suit jacket hanging off the back of a chair and snag it.

"These people you work with, they get you information, right? Like my case?" She fixes the strap of her dress when it starts to slide down her shoulder. "You looked it up."

I grin.

"I did." I slide my arms through my suit jacket, fixing the collar once it's on. I check the time. "We should get going. Jimmy's usually done by ten, and we want to be there before then."

"Did you check on the girls? Is Charlie all right? Her sister?" she asks after the elevator doors slide closed.

"Casper called while you were in the shower. They're doing well. Jackie has three broken ribs. There was some internal bleeding, but they seem to have it under control. She'll be okay." I pick up her hand. "If we hadn't gotten there when we did, she wouldn't have been. Add another day, and they all would have been gone."

"We should have asked Artie if he was holding any girls." She frowns. The blame will not sit on her shoulders, I won't allow it.

The elevator dings, and I lead her off and toward the garage.

"We would have found them a little sooner, but it wouldn't have changed what he'd already done to them." The back lights of my car light up when I hit the fob's button. "What happened to them is his sin, it's Vince's sin, it's Jimmy's sin. You don't carry any of that." I open the car door for her to climb inside.

"Do you understand, Harley? You're not to blame. Not for them. And not for you and your sister." I fix the seatbelt for her so it's not cutting across her throat. She drags in a slow breath, and I wait. I'll wait all night, if I have to, for her response.

"I know." She turns those soft brown eyes on me, and I'm even more hooked than I was before.

"Good," I say, shutting her door.

As I drive, I rest my hand on her thigh, drumming my fingers. Every now and then I squeeze, wishing I had her naked beneath me in bed. But we have all night for that. Once we get home.

"Did they call the police? The people at the hospital?" She breaks the silence when we're halfway into the drive.

"No. Casper said the doctors wanted to, but Charlie made it clear they wouldn't be talking to the cops." I hit the signal and merge onto the highway.

"But doesn't the hospital have to when people come in with those sorts of injuries?"

"Casper took care of it," I assure her.

She grabs her phone that's charging in the middle console.

"It's Mom again. She's worried because I haven't answered her."

"You two talk almost every day." They were close, almost too dependent on each other, up until now.

"Yeah." She cradles the phone in her lap. "I can't talk to her, Zack. I can't even think about her without feeling like I'm going to puke." She sighs.

"We need to talk with her at some point, Harley. Get a clear picture of exactly what went down." It's a gentle warning. Nancy can't go unchecked. Not after the betrayal.

"I know." She picks up the phone again. "I'll just tell her I'll call tomorrow?"

"Sure." I nod while merging off the expressway. "You need some time to figure out what you want to do."

"What I want to do?" She types out her response to her mom, then plugs the phone back into the charger.

"We'll do whatever you decide. She's your mother. It's going to be your call." The woman deserves to burn at the stake. A low fire that slowly eats away at her skin until she falls unconscious. Then a little Middle Ages justice would work well for the rest. The rack, a disembowelment. Any slow and painful end.

But in the end, it will be up to Harley to decide. It has to come from her, so the wounds finally heal. And she can spread her wings to their fullest.

"All those years of worrying about her. Making sure I didn't do anything that would remind her of Quinn too much."

I squeeze her knee.

"I became a teacher because I wanted to make her proud, and she was always telling me how great it would be if I went into teaching. Every decision I ever made was based on how it would make her happy, or proud."

"Harley, there's no right or wrong decision here. Whatever you want is what will happen. You can worry about it later."

"She wanted me dead. I can't just forgive that, right? She

was there. They kept her in one of those offices, but she knew, she saw. And when they did bring her to sit with us, she was never hurt. They weren't doing anything to her, only to us. Like she'd given them the okay." The pain of it sours her tone. She presses her hand to her chest and leans forward, sucking in air. "Quinn screamed for her."

All I can do is let her work through the memory as it hits her. The brain only hides what the soul can't handle. It's a good sign of her strength that the memories are coming back, but it comes at a price.

Slowly, she calms down. She leans back against the headrest and draws in a deep breath. Her chest rises and falls as she gets her anxiety back under control.

"Better?" I ask when she opens her eyes again. The panic is gone, but her face is a little red.

"Yes. I'm sorry."

I touch her cheek.

"No need." The light turns green, and I make a turn. "We're almost there. Five more minutes."

―――

The entrance to the club is in a back alley. Once inside the foyer, I pull out the passcodes Jeff sent me to both access the building and get us access to the elevator for the club. The doors slide open after I punch in the code.

Once we're in the elevator, she giggles.

"Sorry. It's just, that was all very spy movie." She rolls her shoulders back.

I sweep her hand into my mine, taking note of how small it is. She looks fragile, this little bird of mine, but I know her, the real her. She's full of strength and beauty.

"When we get up to the club, just remember not to look at anyone in the eyes. Understand? It's important. You're with me, and if you look at them, they'll think they can take you."

"Take me? Like just pick me up and walk away?" Her anxiety has waned into playfulness. It's fucking adorable, but this isn't the time.

I squeeze her hand. "It's important, Harley. This is a dangerous place; these are dangerous people."

Her eyes darken. "Maybe they should be afraid of us then."

I can't help but smile.

The woman I found with her nose in a book has surprised me.

And not many people do anymore.

"They should. But we can't do anything while we're here. We're going to get him alone, but to do that, we have to pretend we're into all this crazy shit. So do as I say. Do not look at anyone."

"All right, Zack. Don't look at anyone, only you, and do exactly as you say." She nods.

"Yes. And one more thing." I squeeze her hand tightly, needing her to heed this part even more. "No matter what you hear me say in regard to you, remember that I will never let anything bad happen to you. I will protect you."

"I know that, Zack." She turns a trusting gaze up at me.

"Even if it sounds scary. I need you to trust me. Do you think you can do that?" It's a lot that I'm asking of her. Hopefully not too much.

She grips my hand tighter. "I trust you, Zack. No matter what you say in there, I'll go along with it."

My perfect little bird.

"Good girl."

The elevator dings our arrival and I straighten, dropping her hand and moving my toy bag to my other side.

Music with a fast, hard beat envelops us as the doors slide open. I step out first, waiting for her to come off the elevator before I continue on. She dutifully stays two steps behind me, to my left. Sweeping my attention across the club, I'm able to keep her in my view while searching through the crowd.

Security guards stand off to the sides, in corners of the room. No one questions if we belong here. As far as they're concerned, having the passcodes is proof enough. Besides, if I'm a threat, they have enough politicians and judges in their pockets to get whatever trouble I might bring with me washed away.

Fucking sick.

This part of the club, the prelude to the real activities happening behind the door I'm leading us to, is intimate. The striking black dance floor, coupled with the mirrored ceiling, creates the illusion of space and glamour. Plush, black leather couches with red velvet cushions line the outer walls of the club.

We're passing the black marble bar with red under-lighting, when someone steps off the dance floor, bumping into Harley. She knocks into me and bounces off, nearly falling to the floor before I grab her arm and steady her.

"Watch yourself," I snap at her, then turn my gaze to the woman who caused the accident. A man hurries to her side.

"I'm sorry. She wasn't paying attention." He grabs hold of his woman's arm and yanks her to his side. "Apologize," he demands, shaking her.

"I'm — I'm sorry," she stutters, her gaze flittering away from me and landing on Harley.

Harley looks to me, waiting for my direction.

Such a perfect girl.

I give her a nod.

"It's all right. Just an accident," she says, then turns back toward me, keeping her eyes down.

The man drags his woman back into the crowd, and I lead Harley to the main entrance of the real club.

"You're doing wonderfully, little bird," I whisper to her as I pull her in front of me and to the other side.

She keeps her eyes lowered, but I catch her proud smile.

As soon as I reach for the handle on the door, it's yanked open and a man three times my size fills the opening.

"Need something?" He folds his arms over his chest. Very bodyguard-like of him. I wonder if he understands the art of subtlety at all.

"Yes. I need a potato and a fork." I utter the last ridiculous passcode. I had thought Jeff was making a joke when he shot me a text just before we left. These idiots depend too heavily on their little codes.

The bouncer drops his arms and steps aside.

"Welcome." He holds the door for us as we enter. Harley's fear is ramping up. I can sense her, smell it on her. And if I can, others here will too.

I step to the side, letting her come to stand beside me.

Grabbing her arm, I pull her close and lean down to her ear.

"You're doing great, Harley. I know you're scared, but can you be my strong girl and keep it up?" I keep my features stoic, just in case anyone is watching us.

"Don't speak. Nod if you're all right," I order her.

She licks her lip, then gives me the sign.

"You're going to be well rewarded," I promise her. I wish I could kiss her, release some of her fear. But I need to remain aloof. For both of our safety.

This part of the club is more open, and a much larger space. And it needs it.

There are three bar lounges, all set up with the same black and red color scheme. But there is no dance floor in here. Instead, there are three platforms that all the bar couches surround.

To the left of us, on a raised platform is a naked woman bound to a St. Andrew's cross. Her head rests against her left arm. Her chest is heaving. Bright red marks cross her chest and her thighs.

A man stands to her side, whispering in her ear. A thin rod is fisted in his hand.

I grit my teeth, reminding myself that safe play isn't the concern of anyone in this club. This place goes far beyond any BDSM club I've ever played in. There is no safe word scheme. No dungeon masters walking around to be certain the submissives aren't harmed.

As we come to the second platform, it becomes even more evident.

The woman on this platform is on her hands and knees. Blood trickles over her sides and pools beneath her on the floor. She's been whipped. No one offers help. They sit in their black leather loungers and watch while sipping drinks.

"That was a harsh one." A man steps up to me. "The idiot went too far too fast. She won't be any good to him the rest of the night."

"She's still alive, isn't she?" I turn to find him staring at me. His graying eyebrow lifts.

"He'll get a good fuck out of her, I'm sure." He laughs and raises a beer bottle to me in greeting. "Baron Barnes is my name. Haven't seen you here before." Is this man for real? He's playing the part of a high-brow aristocrat too well for me to know if it's a joke or if he's locked in some sort of mental break.

"No." I don't offer more. "First time."

"This one yours?" He gestures to Harley, who's standing in the perfect spot where I can see her, but she is out of our way.

"She is."

"Hmmm." If his beady little eyes so much as touch her, I'm going to have to remove them. "Mind if I have a look?"

My teeth snap together.

Play the part for now.

"No. Not at all. But any part of you touches any part of her, and it becomes mine," I warn, and not just for show. I will gladly cut off his fucking finger if it so much as brushes a hair on her arm.

"Girl, step back, lift your chin up," I order her. "Eyes on me," I add so she understands where to look. I can't have her accidentally giving this monster permission to go beyond what I've allowed.

When her eyes meet mine, a shiver runs through my body. Her fear has twisted into pride. So long as she keeps her eyes on me, she has nothing to worry about.

I'm her protector.

"She's got nice tits," the man says, sipping his beer. He walks around her, his fingers flexing. He wants to touch her ass. I almost want him to try.

A scream from behind me scares Harley. She moves her eyes for a moment but brings them right back to me.

"Are you here to play or to sell?" He comes back around her, stepping in front of her like she's not a person.

And here, at a place like this, she's not.

She's product.

"Tonight, play. I'm not quite done with her yet. She has some more use in her before I make back my money." I check my watch. It's nearly nine and Jimmy has a reputation for only staying until ten.

"How much can she take?" Barnes continues his perverted line of questioning.

Her jaw tenses, but she manages to keep her eyes on me. This man is starting to wake the beast inside her.

"Whatever I give." I turn when there's another scream. Heat courses through my veins.

I know that sound. Unadulterated pain. The floor shakes with it.

When I turn, I find exactly what I knew I would.

A woman is bound over a wooden horse. Black splotches already cover the majority of her ass. Her hair curtains her face, and is soaked in blood.

"That's Jimmy," my guide says, pointing at the horrific scene. "He's really used her up." He tsks like he's almost sad about it. "I was hoping to play with her after he was done, but he's gonna finish her."

"Finish her?" I quirk a brow.

"Yeah. He only beats them like that when he's no longer interested. Ah yes, see, there." He points to the knife Jimmy pulls from a black bag at her feet. "He's gonna fuck her and then when he's finished..." He makes a slicing motion across his throat with this thumb. "It's gonna be a blood bath." He laughs. "See. They've already set up for it." He gestures to the bucket that's been placed beneath her head to catch as much of the mess as possible.

As he's enthralled with Jimmy shoving his cock inside the half dead woman, I check in with Harley. She's staring at the scene, and no matter how long I glare at her, I cannot get her attention.

I don't want her to witness this.

If I pull her away, our little guide here, will suspect I give a shit about her. That will make her even more prey.

I reach around him and slap her hand to get her attention, but she still will not move her eyes.

"Three million!" An insistent bellow comes from further behind me. I take the opportunity to step around Barnes and grab her hand.

"Eyes down, dammit," I growl in her ear. "Do not look."

She hesitates, but then slowly she lowers her chin and puts her eyes on the floor.

My chest unclenches.

When I turn back around a man runs to the platform with his hand raised.

"Three million, Jimmy!" he yells, as he reaches the edge of the platform, nearly toppling over onto it when he screeches to a halt. The information that was sent over for me this afternoon explained that stepping onto a platform while someone was engaged in play would be seen as a personal attack. It could cost the man his life.

Jimmy grunts, thrusting fully into the woman, then freezes, looking over at the man who is bent over, sucking in air.

"I will give you three million for her." The man waves his hand again. "Cash. Tonight."

Jimmy looks down at the woman, bloodied, bruised, mostly unconscious.

"Three and a half," he counters the offer.

Onlookers collectively turn to the man still trying to catch his breath. A fresh batch of panic takes over his eyes. They go wide, his cheeks flush.

"Fine!" He nods feverishly. "Just stop. Get away from her." He picks up his foot, ready to step on the platform, but Jimmy points his knife at him with a shake of his head.

"You can have her after I've had my fill. She'll be alive. But I want what's mine first, Chad."

Chad. I try not to roll my eyes. With his blond hair perfectly sculpted around his face and the tailored suit he's wearing; he looks every bit a Chad.

After a nod of acknowledgment, Jimmy goes back to the woman. He pulls out of her pussy and shoves his cock straight into her asshole. She's awake just enough to react to the new invasion with a whimper.

Chad looks ready to rush the platform, but he manages to control himself as Jimmy fucks her harder and harder in the ass.

"Pathetic," Barnes sighs. "She's going to be broken for weeks, maybe longer before Chad can get any real use out of her this way. He's buying a broken horse."

I push my hand into my pocket when I can't stop myself from making a fist. The urge to pull my knife out of my bag and stick it in his throat is getting harder to ignore.

Finally, Jimmy stops thrusting and unleashes a bellow of his own, signaling he's found his release.

The crowd, no longer interested, turn back to each other in

conversation. Even the women who've been kneeling at the feet of their captors, their owners, look somewhat bored now that the scene is over.

"Chad seems to have feelings for her," I comment as he hurries forward and begins to unbind the woman. Jimmy is already finished with the scene and is cleaning off his cock, wiping off the blood covering his dick and thighs.

"Huh. Maybe so." Barnes shakes his head. "So, are you going to play next?" He waggles his eyebrows.

I laugh.

"Not yet. We just got here, and she needs to settle down before I get her up on the cross. Her nerves will have her puking on me, and then I won't have any fun with her." I reach around and grab Harley's arm.

"I understand. It's been a long time since we had a new member."

"Yes." I nod. "Vince Scaletto recommended it." I pretend to look around for him. "Any chance he's here tonight?"

Barnes' grin falters at the edges. Did he really think he'd figure me out, find out that I don't belong here? Fool.

"Vince? No." He takes a step back. "If you'll excuse me. The store for the evening has opened, and I need to go shopping."

I twist around to see where he's looking and find a roped off area where women are standing on boxes. They range in dress from elegant dresses, to lace underwear, to fully nude.

"He's going to buy one of them," Harley whispers behind me after Barnes walks in that direction. I squeeze her arm.

"We'll deal with that later. Right now, we need to follow Jimmy."

"Are we going to talk to him?" she asks quietly. "He might recognize me."

I shouldn't be letting her speak at all, but she's keeping her eyes down and being soft enough that no one is paying us any attention.

"I am. Yes." I gesture to the platform where Jimmy is grabbing his bag and walking away from the battered and bruised woman now lying in Chad's arms.

"And what am I supposed to do?" she asks, a little more snipe to her tone.

I slide my eyes to her.

"Be a good little bird and sit on your perch. Silently."

TWENTY SEVEN

Harley

Jimmy Blackwood has two missing teeth when he grins. I think someone punched him in the mouth, knocking them out.

I wish I could have seen it.

Or better, been the one to do it.

Zack squeezes my arm and I realize I've raised my gaze again. I'm doing my best to keep my eyes on the elegant black tiles of the club, but I can't help my curiosity.

This place is a nightmare dressed up as fantasy.

Some women moan in pleasure while they're touched and fondled by the men walking them around and sitting with them. Others are screaming and crying out in obvious pain from the tortures they endure.

"Down." Zack points at the small cushion beside the lounge chair he's sitting in. I lower myself as elegantly as I can, given the tightness of this dress. "On your knees," he corrects me when I try to cross my legs over.

A quick look around, and I see that none of the women are sitting on their cushions. They are all kneeling. On display for anyone who wants to look.

I quickly move into position, just as Jimmy Blackwood sits down on the lounger across from Zack. He's cleaned up now, with a drink in his hand.

His gaze turns my stomach, but I can't even look up at him to show him how much he disgusts me.

"She won't look at you," Zack says, leaning back in his chair and hooking his foot on his knee. "She's too well trained."

"Hmm." The ice in Jimmy's glass clinks. "I like the trained ones best. I get to break them down and start all over again. It's twice the fun."

I swallow down the bile rising up in my throat.

"I noticed how you have your fun." Zack reaches to me, stroking my hair. Petting me like I'm some dog.

But it works.

My stomach stops clenching and I'm able to concentrate on his touch instead of on the horrifying sounds of woman crying around me.

"Saw that, huh? Too bad Chad ruined it. But three-and-a-half million will buy me three more girls." His glass hits the table between them. "Smart to have your own girl, better than renting from the shop."

"My girl here? Yes." Zack drops his hand from my head.

"Jimmy, sorry to bug you, but we got a guy who's demanding to see you." Their conversation is interrupted by a man in black boots.

I clench my teeth. I need to look up so I can see who's talking.

I hide my fisted hands in my lap.

"Who is it?"

"DeMarco. Says he has the money to pay back the loan, so he doesn't want to go through with the sale."

"DeMarco?" There's a pause. "Too late. That girl was picked up two days ago. Vince had a buyer right away. She's gone."

More bile raises.

"Shit. Okay."

The boots are gone.

"Too bad for him, huh?" Zack says.

Jimmy hesitates a moment then laughs.

"Yeah." His ice clinks against the side of his glass. "Are you waiting on a platform?" he questions, and my back tightens.

"I am." Zack makes a fist in my hair, giving just enough burn that I can fall back into his voice and tune out Jimmy.

"They'll be scrubbing mine down for a while. That bitch bled like a stuck pig when I cut her face." He's laughing. How can a monster like him be allowed to breathe right now? Why aren't we cutting off his face?

My eyes settle on Zack's black bag. A variety of knives are inside, mingled among the toys.

"I saw." Zack twists my hair, and I groan. It takes my focus away from Jimmy, but the injustice of him being allowed to sit here and enjoy a drink while that poor girl is hurting, while Quinn is buried six feet under the ground, while I'm sitting here listening to him, is almost too much.

Pain ridden screams from the platforms behind us make my stomach quake. I can't just kneel here and listen to this. Every one of these fucking men need to burn.

"Please! Jimmy!" A man in a polo shirt and torn jeans rushes to Jimmy's side just as I move to get up from my space.

"Stay." Zack's fingers snap in front of my face. I freeze, but the anger boils just below the surface. It's going to spill out soon.

"Eyes." When I move them, he pats my head. "Trust," he mouths, and the heat comes down to a simmer. Trust him. And I do. More than I hate them.

He won't let them get away with what they're doing. I have to be patient.

"Look. You sold her. Vince had a buyer, she's gone. Nothing I can do," Jimmy's telling the man.

"Can't you call Vince? Maybe get her back?"

Jimmy laughs.

"No, man. She's gone. Like gone, gone. These guys who buy the girls from Vince…I told you what would happen. She's dead, man. Gone." His laugh sends an electric shiver up my spine.

I know that laugh.

I've heard that laugh. It lives in my brain. In my bones.

As soon as my head snaps up, Zack puts his hand around the back of my neck, but I'm not looking away.

Make a choice already. Which one.

It was him.

I lower my eyes before he sees me. Tears roll off my cheek and fall to my dress.

Zack squeezes just enough to remind me I'm safe. He's here. I'm protected.

"Shit. Sorry, Jimmy. He got past us."

"Just get rid of him." Jimmy waves his hand.

The man, now crying, is dragged away.

"Your girl looks ready to play," Jimmy says. His fucking ice clanks in his glass again. I want to shove each piece of it up his ass. The glass, too.

"Soon," Zack agrees. "I've been wanting to take on another girl. This one is good, but I miss breaking her in."

"I get that," Jimmy agrees. "There's the store here, but most of those girls are used goods. Broken in other ways, you know."

"I do."

"I got a guy if you're interested. Vince."

"The one you were just talking about."

"Yeah. Him. He must be busy today, haven't gotten a response back, but I understand he's got three live ones. Brand fucking new. They've had a rough couple of days, but they'll be perfect for what you're looking for. They'll need breaking in."

Zack's muscle tense. His anger rolls off of him, but Jimmy's too enthralled with making a deal to notice.

"How old?" Zack asks.

"Two younger ones, twenty-one, twenty-two, sisters. Then the older one is forty-five. The mom, but I hear she's a looker. I can see if he still has them available."

"I don't know," Zack counters. "Oh, the platform just opened." He moves to stand, grabbing me by the arm and pulling me to my feet. "Let me think about it and I'll let you know. How can I get a hold of you?"

Jimmy leans out to Zack. "Here's my card. Just text that number. I'll let Vince know you're interested."

"Thanks. That would be great." Zack tugs on me, pulling me away from where Jimmy sits, sipping the rest of his drink. I glance over my shoulder, catching his gaze for moment.

It's just for a breath.

But long enough for the evil to resonate.

"Don't fucking look at him." Zack gives me a little shake.

"I hate him," I say. "Why aren't we taking him now?"

Zack halts, yanks me around so I'm facing him.

"People can hear you." The fierce fire of his gaze burns me. I lower my eyes to his chest.

"I hate him, Zack. He's going to leave and we won't find him again," I whisper my worry.

"We're not losing him, Harley. You're going to have to trust me here. I will not let him get away."

And he won't. Inside my bones, I can feel his sincerity. Jimmy Blackwood will not slip through our fingers tonight. "What are you going to do?" I ask, my nerves suddenly on edge.

He yanks off his suit jacket and tosses it to the edge of the platform.

"I'm going to give Jimmy Blackwood a show."

TWENTY EIGHT

Zack

There's a small table on the platform, next to the wooden beam. There are thick black metal rings, at various levels, on all four sides of it. Perfect for binding any sized person.

"Face the pole," I direct her with a jerk of my head. She slides worried eyes over to the rings. "It's all right, little bird," I whisper into her ear. "I'm right here."

She presses her hand to her stomach, drags in a long breath. I leave her to follow my order and drop my toy bag on the little table.

Out of the corner of my eye, I watch her as she takes gentle strides to the wooden beam and faces it, her back to the onlookers who've taken seats around our platform. As I dig out what I want from my bag, I find Barnes sitting front and center with a greedy smile on his fat little face.

But it's not him I give a shit about right now. It's Jimmy, and there he is. Still by the seats we abandoned, enjoying a second drink, and with his eyes firmly on us.

Perfect.

I bring the cuffs over to where Harley stands. She stares

with determination at the wood; at the rings I'm going to bind her to.

"Hands," I order firmly and loudly so our little audience can hear me. She swallows and offers them up to me.

It's quick work, wrapping the leather cuffs around each wrist then linking them together.

"Pretty girl." Standing behind her, I kiss her cheek as I raise her linked hands up to the nearest ring. Using a D-ring, I clip the cuffs to the ring, stretching her beautiful body up enough that she has to rise to her toes to keep from dangling.

It's uncomfortable, but won't hurt her.

"All this hair." I fist her long, red locks, separating the massive bunch into two sections, and flip them over her shoulders so her back is clear.

"Not the dress, Zack. Please," she whispers when my hands go to the neckline.

I chuckle.

"I'll buy you a dozen more." A promise I will enjoy keeping. She deserves all the best things. If I have to sit outside some fancy dressing room while she tries on every dress in every shop on Michigan Avenue, I'll gladly do it, if only to witness the little smiles she gives when she finds something she likes.

With one jerk, I rip the dress, tearing it in half down the middle.

There was a zipper, but our audience isn't in to practicality. They want violence. The more aggressive it is, the louder it is, the harder their cocks get.

I leave her there, her bare back and bare ass exposed to the crowd, with the red dress dangling in tatters from her arms while I go back to my bag and pull out what I need.

Her eyes warm me as I walk back to her. I let the three braided flogger dangle from my hand. Tears already well in her eyes. It's beautiful.

A shame I have to share this with all of these fucking lunatics.

"Spread your legs," I snap my order, and she wiggles them apart as best she can. This makes the binds bite into her wrists more, and makes the entire position more stressful.

I stand to her left. Reaching my hand between her legs, I cup her pussy. The warmth and wetness make my cock hard.

I kiss her cheek once more.

"This is going to hurt like a bitch, little bird," I warn her. The little knots in the braids will bite into her skin. "You're safe with me."

She lowers her eyes and presses her head against the beam.

"I know," she whispers just before I step back from her half naked from.

Her back and ass are unblemished.

They won't be when we're done here.

Pulling my hand back, I clench my jaw, and unleash.

The flogger cracks across her ass.

She screams, throwing her head back. Losing her footing, she dangles for a second before she finds purchase and gets back into position.

Two dark blotches form on her ass where the knots struck.

I take aim.

Strike.

Another scream of pain, but it's one I've come to love from her. A woman kneeling just off the center of the platform sucks in a gasp.

Again, I whip her. Again and again, until I'm nearly out of breath and her cries melt together and I can't distinguish one from another.

Another woman moans from behind me. I follow her concerned gaze to a spot on Harley's back.

The knot broke the skin, just below her shoulder blade.

There's a thin trail of red as the dollop of blood rolls down her back. I catch it with my thumb and bring it to my mouth.

Her cheeks are flushed, her breathing harsh, but she doesn't beg me to stop.

I can't now, even if she wants me to.

Jimmy has moved seats. He's front and center now, watching us.

I'm not nearly as gruesome as his show.

And not just because I love this woman.

And I do.

The intensity of that love guides my hand as I bring the flogger down on her back, her ass, her thighs.

I cover her with sharp strikes. The knots leave welts. They bite into skin, making her bleed.

Her head lolls to the side, and I can see her eyes have rolled back in her head.

She's flying high, my little bird.

Fuck, this woman is so perfect.

I bring the flogger down across her ass once more. The hardest of the lashes, and she bucks back, screaming again.

When I check on her, tears have ruined her make up. Dark lines from her mascara trail down her cheeks.

"You've never been so beautiful." I fist her hair at the scalp and drag her head back, licking her neck from collar bone to chin before I kiss her so deeply, I almost forget we have an audience.

"Almost done. The next part is the hardest. Be my brave girl," I tell her then shove her head away from me and cross the platform.

Jimmy notices me headed to him and leans toward me.

"Your girl looks worn out," he laughs.

"She's warmed up." I look over my shoulder at her. She's brought her feet back together and eased the strain on her wrists. There's going to be bruising though.

"She's well trained, like you said." He tilts his head to look at her again. "Are you done with her?"

I laugh.

"No. She can take a lot more. But I'm not in the mood. She's too complacent with me." I narrow my eyes and lean closer. "You want a crack at her?"

His eyebrows shoot up. He's a little kid being asked if he wants to live in the chocolate factory.

"I enjoy watching her get hurt as much as I love hurting her." My stomach rolls. I may not make it through this lie without vomiting on this creature.

"You saw how I play," he warns.

I nod.

"I did. That's why I'm asking you. But." I move closer to him. "I don't like all the audience bullshit. In private. Just the three of us. You can do whatever the fuck you want, but she has to live. And no permanent scars on her face. She's pretty and I don't want that ruined."

He eyes me for a second, mulling it over.

"Unless you've had your fun already tonight and aren't in the mood?" I start to get back up, like I'm taking away the offer.

"No." He touches my arm. "I'm definitely in the mood. I have a private suite, but it's in the back. Get her. Let's go have some fun." He stands and flexes his fingers, like he's just itching to get his hands on my girl.

"Are we done?" Harley asks softly as I take her down from the beam.

"Not yet, baby." I hold onto her until she finds her footing. Pulling the tattered dress from her body, her entire body is exposed to the onlookers. "Almost done," I encourage her. "Remember what I said earlier, no matter what you hear me say, know that I won't let anyone hurt you."

She nods.

My girl is tired.

It's been a stressful night, and it's about to get worse. Because I still don't know how I'm going to get his ass out of this place without anyone seeing us.

My promise to Jeff about not taking anyone else out tonight other than Jimmy may have to be broken.

After I toss all the toys back into the bag, I put my hand out to her, a signal for her to come to me. And the perfect girl that she is, she slides her hand into mine, lacing our fingers together.

When we step off the platform, Jimmy grins down at her like he's admiring the plate a chef just put in front of him.

"She really is pretty." He lifts a finger to her chin.

Her fingers tighten around mine when he makes contact, but my girl remains strong.

My breath catches. The longer he stares at her, the more chances are he'll recognize her.

Ten years is a long time, but fifty years could pass, and I'd recognize her.

But she wasn't a person to him back then.

No more than she is right now.

He drops his hand and turns to me.

"My private room is this way." He leads us through the club, around play areas, past a woman being held down by three men while a fourth mounts her. Each scene makes Harley tighten her grip on my hand.

When we reach a door that will lead outside the club, Jimmy steps in front of the keypad to punch in his code.

I take the moment to reassure my girl.

"Who is the only one who gets to hurt you, little bird?" I whisper in her ear.

"You." The corners of her mouth kick up just enough for me to see before she drops any emotion from her face and Jimmy opens the door for us.

I squeeze her fingers.

As soon as the door shuts behind us, all the noise from the club is gone. No music, no screaming, no moans. Nothing but thick silence.

"Soundproof," Jimmy says over his shoulder when I look

back at the door. "When I'm back here I don't want to hear all that bullshit."

There's no noise, but there's also something else.

There's no security.

None of his men are stationed back here.

The last security guard was at the door we passed through. And he didn't bat an eye at Jimmy taking two new members through the door.

He can't be this stupid.

He really thinks he's untouchable.

"It's just down here," he says, turning down a second hallway.

And there it is.

His private suite is right across from a fucking elevator.

Unfortunately, this elevator comes with a man large enough to take on any ape in the jungle.

"Marco." Jimmy nods to his guard as he punches another code into the box. "We don't want to be disturbed."

"You got it." Marco gives a curt nod while his eyes slide all over Harley. She tenses beneath his slimy gaze, but keeps her eyes down. He won't see her disgust, but he'll feel mine soon enough.

This entire place is going to be a pet project for me.

Anyone who has set a fucking toe here is on the list.

"Right in here." Jimmy pushes the door open and gestures for us to go inside. I release her hand and gently push her.

"Inside, kneel in the center of the room until he has use for you." I keep my tone brisk.

As soon as the door shuts, Jimmy's phone blares.

"Fuck. Sorry about this." He grabs it and scans the screen. "I need to take this. One second." He answers the call and stalks off to the corner of the room.

Harley finds a spot in the middle of the area and sinks down to her knees on the tiles. There's nothing of comfort in here other than a few leather wingback chairs. I assume those are for the players and not the girls.

"I don't pay you to come up with fucking excuses." Jimmy's voice carries over to us. I stand in front of Harley, petting her hair. Having to be this close to him is dangerous for her. She might tighten up beneath the fear and memories and get herself hurt.

Just being in this room alone with him might be causing her more trauma.

I check my watch.

"Find them," Jimmy snaps. "It's your job to be sure none of this touches me. Calling me with your little complaints isn't doing your job. Just fucking handle, it, Laurens or you'll be the one people can't find." He ends the call and throws his head back, inhaling as deeply as his chest will allow.

Harley moves, and I put my hand on the top of her head to keep her on her knees. Not yet.

She'll get her turn at him, but not just yet.

Now that he's off the phone, we can get started.

Jimmy turns around with a twisted smile on his face.

"I swear to god, women are only good for fucking and birthing heirs." He takes another breath, then claps his hands together. "I guess they're good for some fun too. Why don't you sit over there? I think I'll start where you left off."

His hands are already on his belt as he stalks toward Harley.

I sink into the chair, put my bag down on the floor at my feet, and let it fall open.

By the time he gets to her, his belt swings from his hand and his eyes are determined.

A shiver runs through her body.

My girl is afraid.

But she's being so fucking good, still.

I grab the syringe I made before we left the condo and uncap it.

"What's your name?" he demands.

She tilts her chin up enough to slide her gaze toward me. I have the syringe ready. All I have to do is get behind him before he notices I've moved.

"Harley," she says, pushing her head back and looking him directly in the eyes.

He laughs. "I guess you're not as trained as he says. That's fine. I love beating submission into a woman." He makes a fist, like he's going to strike her, but I strike first.

I lunge at him, sinking the syringe into his shoulder.

He howls and jumps away, but it's too late. Enough of the drug went in; he's gonna be on the ground before he can get away from us.

"What the fuck was that?" He yanks out the needle and inspects it like he can magically see what's running through his veins right now.

"Just a paralyzing agent mixed with a sedative." Harley climbs up to her feet and steps toward him as he wobbles.

"What? Why...why would you...." he shakes his head. The fog is rolling in.

"Marco!" he yells as he falls to his knees.

Harley grabs his hair and yanks his head back.

His eyes are already glassed over.

"Marco can't save you. No one can save you." She throws her fist into his face as hard as she can. Blood splatters out of his nose. Again he howls.

There's beeping on the other side of the door.

Marco's punching in the code.

I grab my bag and dig out the knife I buried at the bottom.

There's one long beep, signaling that Marco has punched the code in correctly, and the door opens.

I'm already waiting.

As soon as the big ape steps ins, I slip out from behind the door and plunge my knife into his neck.

He bellows, more from rage than pain I think, because he manages to swing around at me.

The knife falls out of his neck, hitting the floor with a clatter.

I take a hit to the face and stumble back a few steps before I hit the wall. A second longer and his fist would have been buried in my stomach, but I managed to dodge him.

He comes at me again. I'm ready this time and get a good punch into his side. It's not enough to take him down though.

His fist lands, then mine. Back and forth we go. I throw my shoulder into his stomach, running at him as fast as I can muster. It throws him off his balance and we hit the ground together.

Just as I scramble off of him, he lets out a blood curling scream.

Blood pours out of his neck.

I blink at my knife sticking straight out of his throat.

He gurgles, choking on his blood and probably the blade of the knife.

"He's not going to hurt you anymore." Harley wraps her hand around the hilt of the knife and yanks it free.

I take the knife from her, kissing her wrist as I do. Stepping away from the monster on the ground, I check in on Jimmy.

He's passed out now. Drool slides down his cheek and drips onto the floor.

I wipe the blood off the knife with his shirt then toss it in my bag.

"How are we going to take him downstairs?" she asks. "And how am I going to go outside like this?" She waves her hands over her naked form.

I pull out a long black T-shirt dress and give it to her.

"I need to clean those little cuts on your back, but it's going to have to wait until we get out of here." I brush her hair from her face. "Are you all right?"

Her cheeks are flushed, but her eyes– there is so much life in them.

"I'm fine. I'll be even better once we're done with him." She pulls the dress over her head.

"Good. This guy can stay here, but we need to get Jimmy across the hall into that elevator. It should lead to the alley we came in."

"No one's going to think it's weird, us carrying him?" She tilts her head.

"Helping a drunk friend to my car. It's fine."

I quickly change my shirt as well, before I handle Jimmy.

He's a heavy fucker, but I've carried heavier.

Throwing him over my shoulder, I look back at Harley.

"Get the bag."

"What about..." she looks down the hall toward the club while we're waiting for the elevator.

"Later, little bird. Don't worry. I haven't forgotten them."

The door opens, and we step inside.

One step closer to ending her nightmare.

TWENTY NINE

Harley

"Mom's asking to go to lunch again." I show my phone to Zack.

"That's fine." He nods and pats his lap. "Come sit with me for a few minutes. He's starting to wake up, but let's give him a minute."

I climb into his lap and look at his laptop.

Jimmy's safely tied in the barn. His muscles aren't awake yet, but Zack bound his head to a board so he could see around him.

I smile when his eyes widen, and fear grips him.

"Are you sure no one will find us out here?" I ask, typing a response to my mother. She's going to have to be dealt with soon.

I can't keep hiding from her.

And she's the last link.

But there's a decision to make.

"This was Dustin's place. He used it for his own purposes. Unless someone's looking for him, no one's coming out here." Zack takes my phone from me and scrolls through my mother's worried texts. "I think she's scared something's happened to you," he says then puts the phone on the arm of the couch.

The farmhouse is a bit dusty, but it's comfortable. Zack gave Jimmy a stronger dose than he did Vince, so it took longer for it wear off. Instead of sitting in the barn all night, we came inside.

"She's probably worried she's been caught." I snort. "I just...I don't understand how she could do it. How could sell us to those monsters?"

"I'm not sure she knows, either." He rubs his hand over my back. There're four bandages on it from where the flogger cut into me.

I know we had to put on a show for Jimmy to get him to want to play with me in private, but it served a secondary purpose. The pain distracted me from being so close to the man who killed Quinn.

But that distraction's over.

"If I were ever in that situation, I'd pick me. Let them kill me and save my kids." Any mother would, I think.

"You would. But then again, I think you'd take out the monsters well before it got to that point." He kisses my shoulder.

The humidity is thick tonight.

I've changed into the tank top and jean shorts Zack packed for me. He thinks of everything. There was a second bag in the car just for me. A second change of clothes, two snack bags of Fritos and cool ranch chips – my favorites.

While he drove us out of the city, he held my hand, lighting brushing his thumb over my knuckles as I curled up in the seat. He left me to my thoughts, just silently watching over me while I worked through the horrible memories.

It's so much easier to fight off the demons when your protector lies in wait beside you, ready to slay them should you fall short.

But the thing with Zack is, I don't think I would ever fall short, at least not to him.

To him, I'm perfect.

"You're everything I never knew a man could be," I say to him, running my fingers through his thick hair.

He smiles. "And how many men have you known?"

"Only a few. There was a boyfriend in college, but he hated that I went home every weekend to spend time with Mom. Said I was a baby that wouldn't let go of Mom's apron strings." I laugh. "What an old saying, apron strings."

He arches an eyebrow. "You went home every weekend?"

I nod. "Of course I did. She didn't like being alone. She didn't make me, and she would tell me I didn't need to, but I could tell she was more comfortable when I did."

A frown tugs at his mouth.

"I thought my sister died because Mom chose me. Whatever my mom needed, I wanted to be sure she had me." I curl into his lap, tucking my head into the crook of his neck.

Inhaling the warm spice of him, my nerves calm.

"Tomorrow." He kisses my head. "We'll figure out what to do about her tomorrow."

"Yeah," I sigh. "What about your parents? You never talk about your family." I could use the distraction from the decision I'm not ready to make.

"I don't have a family." He hugs me tightly to him. "My father...." He pauses as though he's not sure how to say what he wants to say. "My father killed my mother when I was seven. He was a drunk, and he came home one night drunker than I'd ever seen before."

I wrap my arms around him. He's always keeping me in one piece, it's my turn now.

"He tripped over one of my toys, and he went to hit me. Mom stopped him, yelled at him to just go sleep it off." His heart beats faster against my chest. "He beat her to death. Right there in the living room."

"You saw it?" I gasp.

"I was hiding under the kitchen table, but I could see through the legs of the chair. He passed out afterwards. The girl who walked me to school in the mornings found them. I was still under the table. Mom was dead. Dad died in prison a year later. A fight broke out and he got what was coming to him." His chest puffs out with a laugh.

"Where did you grow up, then?"

"An aunt took care of me until I was in my teens. Then when she died, I was thrown into the foster system until I was old enough to enlist in the military."

I pull back from him, searching his expression. "I'm sorry your dad did that."

He runs his fingertips over my cheek bone, then touches the tip of my nose.

"Me too, little bird. She was a good woman." He smiles.

I twist around to look at the screen again.

Jimmy fully awake, and making every attempt to get out of the binds, but Zack is too good at what he does. Jimmy won't ever get out.

"Do you want to go play with me?" I whisper.

"Are you ready?" he asks, helping me off his lap and onto the cushion beside him.

I nod.

"Then let's go play."

The barn is lit up with the painter's lights again, but this time instead of Vince, we have Jimmy ready for us.

"Look. I don't understand what's happening, but you don't know who you're fucking with," Jimmy yells, as soon as we step inside.

Zack slides the barn doors shut.

"You really don't remember me, do you?" I step in front of him, bending over to give him a good look at my face.

He searches me, panic growing in his eyes.

"No. Should I?" It's not surprising. This monster has killed numerous women.

We're just faceless things to him. I wonder if he even looked at our faces before pulling that trigger.

I throw on a fake frown. "Harley Turner," I say.

It takes a second, but then it hits him. His eyes widen, his mouth drops. "You're the girl Laurens is looking for."

"I am." I smile. "Do you remember me though?"

His bare chest heaves.

Zack had the foresight to strip the monster before binding him. Makes it easier for us now.

"You're Nancy's kid. The one I didn't kill." His face contorts into disgust. "You two are fucked. You think my cousin is going to let you get away with this?"

Zack laughs.

"Your cousin can do whatever he wants. I don't have any issue with him yet, but you...now you have my attention." Zack hops onto the surgical table. "Don't look at me, though, look at Harley. She's in charge here."

When Jimmy swings his gaze back to me, I strike. Slapping him hard across his face, then throwing my fist into his nose again. There's another crunch, louder than the first one in his playroom.

Fresh blood pours out of his nose. More howling.

I step back from him, looking over the scrawny man sitting naked in front of me. His hands are bound behind him, his ankles are tied to the chair legs. He's completely exposed to me.

Completely vulnerable.

Just as we were when he walked in that day.

"Dad's debt was paid by just one of us, is that right?" I ask him.

He laughs. "Yeah."

"But you had all three of us taken."

"No. Vince had you taken. Arthur wanted to play with you all first, and Vince owed him a favor." He wiggles his head against the leather strap holding him against the chair back.

"But you bought the kill." I walk over to the metal tray Zack has ready for me. All of the instruments I need are there. I run my hand over the knives, the scissors, the miter saw.

"I'd had a bad day," he says. "Needed to relieve some stress."

He's so casual about this, I'm not sure he's taking me seriously.

I pick up a scalpel.

"Do you think this is a game?" I press the blade to his cheek, slicing downward until blood slides down.

"Fuck!" he bellows, jerking against his binds.

"You killed my sister." I move to his disgustingly hairy chest. "You put a gun to her head and shot her." I slice his nipple, and the little bud just pops right off.

"What the fuck!" He sucks in air, trying to combat the pain, but there's no running from it.

"You raped me." I move down to his dick, picking up the flaccid member.

"No! No!" He's trying to move the chair, but he's too weak still. All he can do is watch as I slice off a chunk of his cock and drop it next to his nipple on the floor.

Now he's a howling mess.

"You were going to kill that woman tonight." I bring the scalpel to his throat, cutting just deep enough for it to hurt, but not enough actually harm him. It's nice, this blade. Precise without having to use much force.

"I didn't! I didn't kill her!" Now he's seeing how serious this is. He searches my face, a plea in his eyes.

"Only because that man saved her," I scoff. "If you weren't

sitting on your asshole, I'd stick this up there and cut you in two." I tap the tip of the scalpel against his nose.

I drop the tool back onto the surgical prep table and pick up my knife. The one Zack gave me. I also pick up the pistol and look it over. I've never fired a gun before, but it can't be that hard at close range.

"Zack, do I just pull this thingy back and fire?" I show him the hammer.

He smiles. I'm making him proud; I think. It warms me, the idea that he's proud.

"You got it. When you pull back the hammer, the bullet moves to the chamber. Just aim and shoot then," he explains.

"If I shoot him in the head, there'll be brains everywhere though, right?" I scrunch up my nose. Cleaning up that mess will be disgusting.

"Don't worry about that. Just do what you want," he encourages me. He always encourages. He's my sounding board. My cheerleader.

"Jimmy." I step up to him again. He's lost in his own misery though, sobbing openly. So much for the tough Mafia boss persona he tries to portray.

I roll my eyes.

"Jimmy!" I kick his shin. His attention snaps to me.

"I'm going to give you a choice here. I'm feeling indecisive." I show him the knife and the gun. "You're a dead man. You know it and I do too, but I'm gonna let you decide. Eat a bullet, or a blade?"

Fat tears track down his face through the thick stubble of his five o'clock shadow.

"I have a wife."

"Don't care." I shrug. "She's better off without you. I'm sure of it." I lift my hands. "Decide please."

"Jimmy, she's using her manners, you should cooperate before she loses them and you get whatever hell is coming to you," Zack teases.

Jimmy looks from one of us to the other, then swallows.

"My cousin is going to kill you for this!" he screams, a desperate attempt that I can't blame him for. His life is coming to an end. It's hard to grasp that.

"Doesn't change what's happening here. Now, last chance. Choose. Or I can get my little scalpel back until you do?" I offer a third option. I'll just slice him until he finally cooperates.

A sob breaks through.

"Fine," he sniffs, trying to find courage that doesn't live in his soul. "Gun. I'll eat a bullet." He nods, looking me straight in the eye.

"You're sure?" I ask lifting one hand then the other.

"Yeah. The bullet." He tries to raise his chin, like he's going to go out with some dignity.

I pull back the hammer and aim the pistol at his head, stepping as close as I need to until the barrel is almost touching his forehead.

He shuts his eyes, resolved, I guess, for what's coming.

I laugh.

How can I not?

This idiot.

His eyes fly open.

"You didn't think I'd actually let you choose? Did you?" I stab the knife into his stomach, tossing the gun to the floor so I can use two hands. Grabbing the handle, I yank the knife to the side, gutting the bastard. It's hard with all his muscle, but the blade is big enough to cut through. By the time I get to the end of his torso, my arms ache.

His scream cuts off quickly, as his insides become his outsides.

I step back, away from the mess, taking the knife with me.

Zack hops off the table and comes stand beside me, his arm around my waist.

"You did good, little bird." He kisses my temple.

"It felt good."

THIRTY

Zack

"The cement truck finished an hour ago. Demolition will take place tomorrow, after the cement has had time to cure," Jeff reports.

"Good. Thank you for taking care of that. I know none of this was official." Dustin's barn came in handy. Everyone fit nice and snug in his pit. After the concrete cures, they'll all be part of the foundation. Of course, all identifying material– like teeth and fingerprints– were removed before the fill in took place.

He laughs. "Fuck, man. Nothing we do is official." He pauses. "Thought you might like to know Casper found a link between those girls you rescued and a guy name Baron Barnes. He's taking care of it."

"Really?" I'll have to call Casper, see if he needs any help with the Baron. The fucker's eyes touched my girl, he shouldn't get to keep them.

"Yeah. Looks like he was the buyer. Vince hadn't gotten in touch with Jimmy about it, yet. Found it on Vince's phone. That fucker really was stupid. He never erased any messages."

"Maybe he thought he could use them as a safety net in case he got busted and needed something to get him out of trouble." Or he was just a complete moron.

"Well, whatever the reason, we have them all. A complete list of buyers and sellers, names of girls, locations of pickups." Jeff sighs. "He's done most of my work for me. Thanks for getting that phone over as fast as you did."

"Not a problem. Do the girls know?"

"What Casper's doing? No. They don't know about the buyer. He wants them to heal up."

"They're doing all right then?" Harley will want to know they're safe and sound.

"As good as they can, I guess. Charlie's already asking about the boyfriend," Jeff huffs. "Casper's assured her he won't go unpunished."

"Casper's taken an interest in her?" Harley walks through the bedroom after her shower with only a towel on her head.

"Seems like it. Sort of like you, huh?" He laughs.

"I don't have an interest." My eyes never leave her naked body as she saunters around my bedroom, plucking up a pair of panties and a tank top from her bag. The marks from my flogger still paint her ass and parts of her shoulders. The cuts from it have healed enough that we can leave the bandages off today.

"So this girl you've been working with, she's nothing?"

"She's everything, Jeff." Each word is enunciated with force.

"We'll need to add her if you want her to get paid at some point. I'm assuming you'll be keeping her around?"

I watch my little bird slide the pink cotton panties up her marred legs, over her supple ass and the perfect curves of her hips, with pure desire.

"It will be up to her." I won't cage her. Everything in her life will be her choice. No one will ever choose her path for her again. Not if I have anything to say about it.

"Just let me know when the time comes. You have the address you needed. Do you need anything else?"

"No." Steady steps bring me to Harley as she watches me in the full-length mirror. A pair of cutoffs dangle from her left hand. I shake my head, and she drops them to the floor. A knowing smile hits her lips.

"Shouldn't need you for a while," I say, trailing my fingertip over her shoulder, pushing the thin strap of her tank top down.

"Let me know if that changes." He ends the call and I toss my phone onto the bed.

"Was that Alfred?" she asks, still looking at me through the mirror.

"Alfred?" I cock an eyebrow.

"Yeah, the old guy who stays in the Batcave and does all the tech stuff?" She giggles slightly at her own wit.

"You still think I'm some caped hero?" Pushing the second strap down her shoulder, I shove the tank down further until her breasts, perfect and round, pop out.

"No." Water from her wet hair flies when she shakes her head. "I think you're more like a dark knight." She tilts her head to the side as I lean into her, giving me full access to her neck.

I kiss her there, just where her shoulder ends. While I'm here, I scrape my teeth along the sensitive spot before biting down.

She hisses a little, reaching her hand up and resting it on my cheek while I bite my way down her throat, over her shoulder.

"Are you well-rested, little bird?" I wrap my arm around her middle and pull her into my body so she can feel how hard she makes me.

"I am." She pushes her ass back into me.

"Hmmm." Sliding my hand along her stomach, I dip my

fingers below the elastic of her panties. Her pussy is soaked already for me.

"Bend over for me. Hands on the mirror." I shove my jeans down, fisting my cock. I've never been so hungry.

She complies, like the good girl she is.

For me.

Anyone who crosses her, they'll find how bad she can be.

"Watch us in the mirror." I pull the slip of fabric to the side, giving me full access to her beautiful pussy.

Her face bursts into a blush and I think I may die the best death there is.

"If you move your eyes away, you'll go days before I let you come again." It's a threat I'm happy to make good on. Keeping her on edge for days, while I torment her over and over again, would be more fun than a man like me deserves.

But she makes me feel worthy.

The way she looks at me, like I really am a hero, breathes life in a soul I thought had dried up long ago.

"That sounds horrible." She fakes a frown and I slap her ass.

"It would be for you." I punctuate my sentence by thrusting into her sweet pussy.

Her eyes hold mine in the mirror as I pound into her, over and over again. Each thrust jiggles her breasts. No sense in denying myself. I reach around her, cupping each breast before I pinch her nipples, pulling them down hard.

She still manages to keep her eyes on me while she whimpers and whines from the torment I deliver.

Fuck, this woman is perfect.

After a few moments, I let go of her, letting the blood rush back into the starved peaks. Again, she hisses, but her eyes never falter.

She arches her back. The new angle sucks me in deeper, making the passage even tighter.

My balls pull tight.

The familiar zing of arousal speeds down my spine.

"Fuck." I thrust harder.

Her swollen clit drips with her arousal when my fingers find it again. Rolling it between my fingers, pressing down just on the top, just like she loves, and she's bucking back at me with a pitched fever.

But her eyes never leave me.

"Fuck. Fuck." My mouth drops open. It's all too much, but still not enough. I could fuck this woman every day for the rest of my life, and it wouldn't be enough.

"Oh!" She slaps the mirror. "Can I? Please?" she begs me for her release.

Just when I thought she couldn't get more perfect.

She does.

"Yes. Oh, fuck yes." I increase the pressure on her clit, driving harder into her pussy until we are both crying out with our release.

I thrust again and once more, then still.

She drops her head between her arms, sucking in air.

Her arms shake from holding the position I put her in.

Slowly, I withdraw from her, putting her panties back in place and help her stand straight again.

Turning her around to face me, I pull up her tank top, stopping a moment to place a kiss over our initials. It's faint now, but it will be there for a long time, I think.

After I have my jeans back on, and she's dressed herself in her jeans and tank top, I pull her to the armchair and sit her in my lap.

She nestles her head beneath my chin, and we cuddle.

"After tonight, when this is all done, are you going to leave?" Fear shakes her voice.

I squeeze her tighter.

"That depends."

"On what?" She runs her fingertips up and down my arm.

"If you're ready to leave Chicago, or if you need some time here."

She pulls back to look at me. There's a little wrinkle in her forehead pulling her eyebrows down.

"You want me to go with you?"

I touch the thin scar of our initials.

"I told you, you're mine now." I kiss her softly.

"What if you change your mind when all this is done, and there's no more danger?"

I chuckle.

"Why's that funny?" She cocks her head.

"Because you think loving someone isn't dangerous?" I kiss her again, a soft peck.

"You love me." No doubt lingers in her words or in her soft brown eyes. "I was afraid..."

I knuckle her chin until she looks up at me again.

"You were afraid I didn't love you back?"

She chews on the inside of her lip for a moment.

"When did you know?"

"You stabbed Jimmy's guard for me." I tuck her wet hair behind her ears. "We're going to spend forever protecting each other, just like that."

She sighs happily and tucks herself beneath my chin again.

"But first, we have finish what we started here," she says softly.

"Yes." I nod. "When you're ready."

Her body tenses in preparation.

"I'm ready, Zack. Let's finish what we started."

THIRTY ONE

Zack

Special Agent Laurens lives in a two-bedroom ranch in the western suburbs. Potted flowers decorate her porch. A garden gnome stands guard beneath a maple tree in the front yard.

"What if she's not home?" Harley questions as we make our way up the walkway to her front door.

"She's home," I assure her, pointing to the window on the garage. "Her car's here."

Harley rings the doorbell, then steps back to my side.

"Are you sure this will work?" she asks while we wait.

"It will." I move the bag from my right hand to my left, then push the doorbell again. There're no cameras.

Not surprising for a dirty cop, but stupid, considering she can't see who's at her door from the safety of inside.

"See? She's not here." Harley gestures to the door.

"She's here," I say, opening the screen door and pounding on the interior door.

A moment later, the doorknob turns.

"Her doorbell must have been broken." Harley tenses besides me.

Special Agent Laurens opens the door in a pair of black yoga pants and a bright yellow workout tank. Sweat drips down the side of her face.

We've interrupted her workout.

The flush from the exertion of whatever routine she was doing drains from her face when she sees us standing on her porch.

She blinks, then quickly composes herself.

"Harley." She shoves on a plastic smile. "What are you doing here?" Her concerned eyes move to me, then to my bag.

"I'm sorry to bug you on a Saturday, but I remembered some other things, and I needed to talk to you." She reaches for the screen door, but Laurens grabs the handle from the inside, holding it closed.

"Mom gave me your address," Harley says. "I really need to tell you about it. Do you mind if we come in?" Harley drops her hand from the door, giving Laurens the impression that she has a say in whether or not we go inside.

There is no choice here, but she doesn't fully comprehend the situation.

As far as she knows, people she works for, and with, have gone missing. There's no proof any of them are dead. And there never will be. So, she has only suspicion.

And nothing to back up the idea that we're behind any of it.

"We'll only be a few minutes. We have dinner plans with her mom." I make a show of checking my watch. "We only have about an hour before we have to be there. It'll take almost that long to get there." Laurens lives on the outskirts of the city.

Laurens relaxes.

"Okay. Yeah. But really, just a few minutes." She pushes the screen door open, letting us inside her sanctuary.

"Let's go in the living room." After shutting the door behind us, she leads us to the small room just off the foyer.

It's a standard living room. A couch faces a flat-screen television and is pushed back against a wall. Over the couch hangs a painting of some Italian village. A vase of flowers sits in the middle of the coffee table.

All normal for a suburban home.

The coffee table is pushed back and there's a workout video paused on the TV screen. Pilates.

Typical.

"Have a seat." She gestures to the couch.

"I'd rather stand, if that's okay?" Harley says, and I take a seat in an armchair in the corner. I'm not needed yet, so I'll just stay out of the way.

"Yeah. That's fine." She sinks into the couch herself. "I did some looking and there wasn't anything about an Arthur in the files. If you want, I can schedule some time to talk with your mom this week, see if she remembers something." She frowns. "Today's the day, right? I don't want to push her about this until after, unless you think I should?" She glances at me in the corner before facing Harley again.

"Today is the day," Harley says firmly. "Quinn was shot on this day, eleven years ago." She plays with her purse strap that hangs diagonally across her torso, sliding her hand down to the bag at her hip.

"Yes." Laurens leans forward, gripping her hands together. "I'm sorry, Harley, I know today is such a bad day for you and your mom. If you'd rather we talk about this some other time, I understand."

"No." Harley shakes her head. "Today's fine." She swallows, rolls her shoulders back.

"Okay. What is it you wanted to tell me?"

Harley sets her jaw.

"I know what you did."

"What I did?" Laurens tilts her head, still playing the oblivious fool. "Did what?"

"I know you work for the Blackwood family, hiding their

crimes, diverting any investigations that might come up. You're on their payroll," she says firmly. It's a beautiful scene, watching her take back power from those that stole it from her.

I'm a lucky man, getting to watch my little bird find her wings.

"Harley," Laurens laughs her name. "I don't know who's been telling you this, but they're wrong." She shoots me a glare. "Is it you? Have you been lying to her?"

I smile.

"I don't tolerate lying, Special Agent Laurens. I would never do such a thing." I put my bag down at my feet on the soft beige carpeting.

Her gaze slides to the bag.

"I don't know what you're talking about, Harley. I haven't done anything other than try to find the men responsible for your sister's death." Her denial is flat, rehearsed. And maybe someone with a less trained ear for such bullshit would believe her. But she's not good at her job. Any of them.

As she makes her denial, her gaze flicks to a case sitting on the bookshelves next to the television. Her gun is probably inside. One of them, anyway.

"You never did a real investigation into our case. You pretended, took statements from me, questioned me every now and then, hoping I hadn't remembered what really happened." Harley takes a small step forward. "And it wasn't that hard to let it go unsolved. We were dumped at a hospital. Quinn's body, too. Nothing linked us to that mechanic's shop."

Laurens' face contorts with that little fact.

I get up from my seat, moving behind Harley while she continues to lead the scene. Such a powerful woman, my girl.

"No physical evidence, only my fucked-up memory, and Mom didn't know anything." She pauses. "That should have been a flag to me. How could Mom not have known anything about who kept us prisoner?" she huffs.

"Harley." Laurens rubs her hands against her knees. "I

know this is all confusing. Your memories are starting to come back, obviously, and it's all messed up. I think you should see a doctor. A therapist who can help you sort it all out." She reaches for her cell phone on the coffee table, but Harley's quick.

She snatches it up first and tosses it to me.

"What are you doing?" Laurens barks at me. I pocket her phone, then flip open the wooden box she keeps eyeing. Sure enough, there it is.

"I don't think a therapist is going to help much." Harley twists toward me, smiling when she sees the gun. "I think that would work best," she says to me with her hand out. The Glock in her purse, the one I took off the security guard at Jimmy's place, can stay tucked away.

She's right, Laurens' own gun is best.

"Harley!" She sits back on the couch, flittering her eyes to me. "What are you doing? Please. You need help. You've got this all twisted."

"She's helping herself," I tell her. "You're a dirty cop who helps monsters steal little girls and women. You help them get away with the worst things imaginable."

"Look. It's not my fault. I had to. You don't understand."

"I do understand." Harley pulls back the slide. "You probably had a good reason at the beginning. Maybe they were blackmailing you, or you needed money, or whatever. I don't care.

My sister and I were beaten, raped repeatedly, and then my sister was killed. That's what I know. That's what I care about."

She aims.

"Harley, please. I can help you." The begging begins. "I'll open a real investigation. We'll get them all." Special Agent Laurens offers what she cannot give.

"There's no need for that," I say. "We've already taken care of them."

Laurens' eyes widen. Fear rolls off of her.

"Please, I'm sorry. So, so–"

The bullet strikes Special Agent Laurens in the forehead. Her lifeless body slumps back, the back of her head splattered against the wall.

"I couldn't listen to her anymore." Harley drops her hand to her side with a frown. "All the lying and the begging. It's just annoying."

"True." Bringing my bag to the coffee table, I pull out a pair of latex gloves. "Let me have it." I wiggle my fingers at the gun in Harley's hands.

"What are you going to do?" She peeks into the bag as I pull out a rag to wipe off all of her prints. "What's that?" She points at an insulated lunch box that's inside the duffel bag.

"We need to replace your prints." I open the lid of the box and pull out Jimmy Blackwood's hand.

"Oh. Ew." Harley takes a step back. "It stinks." She covers her nose.

"Of course it does." I laugh. "I've preserved it as best I can with ice packs, but decomposition is going to smell.

Carefully, I wrap his hand around the gun. Pressing his fingers in all the right spots. Once I'm satisfied with my work with the weapon, I go to work placing fingerprints on the coffee table and on the glass of water sitting beside the flower arrangement.

"Won't it look sloppy, leaving the gun behind?" Harley asks when I drop it in on the couch beside her.

"Maybe, but she's a dirty cop and he's in the Mafia. What better way to close this case fast than to pin it on a mobster?" I close the box, zip up the bag and gesture toward the front door. "Are you ready?"

She chews on her lips.

The next stop is the worst stop.

But this has to draw to a close.

She takes in a deep breath, rolls her shoulders back, and gives a firm nod like she's made her decision.

"As ready as I'm going to be." She heads to the door. "Let's get it over with."

THIRTY TWO

Harley

Fading evening sun rays beat down on us as we stand at edge of Mom's lawn. Zack's strong hand holds mine as a tremor runs through my body.

"We don't have to do this," he reminds me.

"It's all right." I take in a breath. "This has to be finished." I squeeze his hand. "So our future can begin."

The front door swings open and Mom hurries onto the porch.

"Harley! Honey!" She smiles wide, her arms spread out in welcome. "I was afraid you wouldn't make it."

I let go of Zack's hand and climb up the steps into Mom's waiting arms. She wraps herself around me, hugging me tightly and swaying just a bit.

"I'm so glad you came. I've been worried about you," she says, patting my back before pulling away. "Come in. I have dinner all ready."

I follow her inside, holding the door for Zack until he grabs it from me.

Lasagna.

I inhale the scent of my childhood.

Mom made lasagna on our birthday every year. It was the one meal we both loved.

"Come in the kitchen, I just need to mix the salad." She leads us through the house to the kitchen in the back.

The lasagna sits on the stove, steam still rising from the dish. I inhale, letting the warmth of my childhood rush over me.

When I open my eyes, Mom's staring at me.

"Honey?" She picks up my hand and squeezes. "It's a shit day, I know."

A tear slides down my cheek before I can stop it.

"I'm sorry." I wipe it away.

"No, don't apologize." She hugs me again. "Sit, I'll get some wine." She smiles and hurries over to the bottle sitting on the counter.

"I'll open it." Zack takes the bottle opener from her. "Why don't you two sit and I'll pour."

"Oh. Sure. Thanks." She steps away from the counter and watches me warily while she sits at the round table.

The same table where Quinn and I ate breakfast every morning with my father before he went to work.

The same table where we ate dinner with my mother, trying not to stare at the empty seat my father left after he died

The same table where my mother and I ate silently for years, pretending there weren't two empty chairs after Quinn died.

"Did you visit the cemetery today?" Mom asks after several moments tick by.

"No," I breathe. "Did you?"

"I did." She nods. "I put out a new basket of flowers for your sister, and left a cigar for your dad." A whisper of a smile touches her lips. "I was going to ask you to come with me, but you've been so hard to get in touch with lately." She eyes Zack.

Zack pops the cork out of the bottle of white wine and pours two glasses.

"Mom." I grab her hands in mine. When did they get so thin? She's always been lean, but all I can feel now is her bones.

"What is it?" she asks when I stay silent. "Oh, thank you, Zack." She leans back, letting Zack place the wine on the table between us.

"My memory is back," I say quietly. "All of it."

Her hands tense.

"I know what...what you meant when you said my name that day."

Her cheeks blanche.

"Oh. Harley." She sinks back in her chair, slowly letting go of my hands. "I...was afraid that's what was happening."

"Is that why you called Agent Laurens? You figured if I remembered one thing, everything was coming back, and she needed to be warned?" I do my best to temper my tone, but the accusation stands on its own.

"No. I...I'm not sure what you want me to say, Harley." She drops her hands into her lap. "Today is–"

"Your fault." I raise my chin. "Dad's fault, too. But you... you gave me and Quinn to those men."

"No." She shakes her head. "That's not how it happened," she says with force. Her eyes harden. "I tried. I did. To save you both."

"You were barely in the room with us, and when you were, you were fine. They never touched you. Only me and Quinn!" I slam my hand on the table. The lies. So many over the years. I've had my full of them. There's no more room in my soul to hold them.

"They kept me in the office. Yes." She nods, side-eyeing Zack. "Is he doing this? Is he putting these horrible ideas in your head?"

Zack leans against the counter, one foot casually hooked

over the other, his arms folded over his chest. He's just listening. All the room in here is for me. He's not crowding any of the space.

"No. I remember. I remember screaming for you. I remember Quinn crying for you." Tears choke me.

"You think those sounds don't haunt me every day?" Her voice cracks. "They didn't have me in the same room with you because they had me tied up in the office. They had cameras on you, and they forced me to watch—" A sob breaks through. "They made me watch the terrible things they did and if I refused, they would hurt both of you."

I shake my head, unsure where to put this information.

"They broke Quinn's nose," she blurts. "They were hurting you, and I refused to watch. I shut my eyes and I starting humming really loud so I couldn't hear you crying. And they went out and punched her so hard in the face, blood squirted out of her nose." A sob breaks from her chest. It's filled with agony, pure agony.

She's not faking this.

"Your husband took out a loan with Jimmy Blackwood." Zack cuts in when I'm too shaken to speak.

"Yes." Mom nods. "He did. The medical bills were killing us. They were going to take the house, our car. There was no hope, he knew that. So, he took the money."

My heart clenches.

"I agreed to be the collateral, knowing I could never make the payments. I figured you and your sister would go live with Aunt Phyllis in California when it was done. You'd be together." She sniffs. "I was so scared, so unsure of what to do. And I loved him so much. The idea of living without him...of not being able to take care of you two...." She shakes her head, like she can get rid of it all. "You would have been together."

"Aunt Phyllis? She died, Mom." I find the flaw in her lie.

She frowns. "Yes, she did. I found out she died the day

before they came for me. I begged them to let me find another way."

The pain balloons in my chest. "You did. Us."

"No!" She hits the table. "Do you think those people are reasonable? When I begged for another way, they said sure... they barged into the house, they kidnapped all three of us. I had no say, no control after that."

I close my eyes, letting the horrible images from years ago bombard me.

Mom screaming as three men pushed past her into the living room where Quinn and I were watching music videos.

"They didn't hurt you though, only us."

"Just because I didn't tell you about what they did, doesn't mean they didn't do it," she says coldly.

Zack stands behind me, squeezing my shoulders.

"You knew Agent Laurens was dirty." I move on. The memories are too strong, too vivid now.

"I did. She met us at the hospital, she did a good job of pretending to care. But when we were home, she came over and explained how things needed to go to keep you safe."

"Me?"

"In some ways, Harley, I've never left that room. When you lost the memories, it was a gift. If you had spoken up, if I had told the truth, they would have gotten to you."

"Isn't that what you wanted?" I shout. "You told them to kill me!"

She grabs my hands, holds tight. "No! Don't you remember? I told them I choose me. I chose me!"

"Quinn, honey, you have to stay awake, baby. Please," Mom begged Quinn to wake up. But she was too deep in sleep to hear her. I scooted across the cement as much as my chains would allow and tried to tap her arm. But nothing.

"She's tired, Mom. I think they hurt her pretty bad last time." I linked my fingers with hers. She'd been so bruised when they brought her back and dumped her next to me. Her face was swollen and purple on one side.

Mom sniffled.

"I can't believe this is happening." She folded herself into herself, resting her head on the knees.

The door opened and a second later, the overhead lights flickered to life. I squinted; the light was too bright. It hurt.

"Hello, ladies." A voice I hadn't heard before greeted us. He sounded so happy, like a game was about to start.

"Please. No more," Mom whimpered. *"Don't touch them."*

"Don't worry, Mommy dearest. I won't." Jimmy pulled a chair in front of Quinn and me. Sitting backwards on it, he rested his chin on the chair back. *"Looks like they've been all used up already anyway."* He frowned at Quinn. *"She still breathing?"*

"I am." Quinn shoved her hands against the cement and pushed herself back up, turning her battered face to him. Relief washed over me. She hadn't spoken since they tossed her back in her spot hours ago.

"Good." He pulled a gun from the back of his jeans. *"Unfortunately, your time is up. We need the room for fresh product."*

"Product?" I looked behind him. Arthur stood at the doorway, a sinister grin on his lips.

"Yeah. We were going to wait until the price went up a little more, but you know, I really fucking need this today." He pointed the gun at Quinn. I tried to jump in front of her, but the chains on my ankle kept me just out of reach.

Jimmy laughed.

"Fuck, you are a stupid bitch, aren't you? How long you been here, and you still don't know you can't get to each other?"

"Leave them alone. Just take me," Mom whimpered. *"Just take me!"* she yelled.

Jimmy's eyebrows lifted.

"What would the fun be in that?" He laughed again. "But look. I've got somewhere I need to be, so let's just get right to it." He stood up, pushed away the rolling chair and stood between Quinn and me. *"Mom, it's time."*

"For what?" She jumped to her feet. "What are you doing?"

"Which one?" He moved the gun from Quinn to me then back again. "Which one do you want to keep?"

"No!" She tugged on the chains. "Me. Take me. I choose me!" She waved her arms in the air. "Take me!"

"Sorry." He shrugged. "That's not an option. But if you keep fucking with me, I can have my guys come out here and have another go at them."

Mom sank to her knees, sobs wracking her back.

"No. Please. No more."

"That's what I'm saying. This can end now." He motioned toward us. "Which one is it?"

Mom lifted her head, stared at us. Tears dripped down her cheeks. She'd aged so much in the time we'd been locked away.

"Forgive me." She whispered; her eyes locked on me. "Harley."

"Good choice." He moved closer.

My chest tightened.

Too many thoughts jammed into my brain at one time. Feelings were out of control.

She said my name.

She chose me.

He pointed the gun at me.

The hammer cocked.

I shut my eyes, crying into my hands.

"Mom!" Quinn yelled.

I sobbed.

"No!" Mom's tortured scream escaped.

BANG

"No! Oh god!" Mom screamed again.

A soft thud beside me.

Slowly, I opened my eyes. Quinn laid on the cement next to me, her blood pooling on the cement, encroaching on me.

Jimmy laughed.

He winked at Mom, who was desperately trying to get to Quinn.

"Huh. That was fun. Good luck with that."

THIRTY THREE

Harley

"You had to choose." My tears soak my shirt. "And you let me believe all these years you chose me to survive."

"Yeah. I did." She nods. "Because how could I have told you differently?"

Silence stretches between us. I was never angry with her for choosing before. I knew she had no choice.

Was I mad now because it was me she chose instead of Quinn? How unfair is that?

"Harley." She scoots closer. "Harley, Quinn was so injured, she wasn't going to live, even if we got to the hospital that minute. I saw what they did to her, honey. They hurt her so badly, there were so much internal injuries and blood loss. Baby, you didn't see all the blood." She sniffles.

"She was going to die anyway, but you still picked me to die too?" How much pain can the heart take before it just stops?

"What they did to you and Quinn. The trauma. I..." She leans back in her chair, tired and pained. "They'd hurt you so much, too. I thought...I thought we would all be better off dead."

I stare at her a long moment.

"I wasn't going to survive losing either of you, I figured if they didn't kill me, I'd handle it myself." She looks to Zack. "You think I'm a monster."

Zack stays somber, silent.

"But you told Laurens about my memory returning. She tried to kill me, Mom."

"I know." She nods. "I...was scared. Jimmy was still making threats after all these years."

"The pension," Zack pipes up.

"Yes," she explains. "He said if I didn't help him with some money issue, he'd find Harley and finish what he started. I didn't understand what he wanted from me, so when those pension papers came, I showed Harley. Only, after she left that night, I understood. They would deposit the money into my account and then they'd withdraw it."

I lean back in my chair.

"Honey, do you understand? Do you believe me?"

I stare at her, exhausted and sick.

"I don't know."

"I swear, baby, I swear I didn't choose you because I didn't love you," she sobs.

"When I started to remember, you should have come clean about everything." I get to my feet.

She wipes her face. "Does she know you remembered everything?" she asks me.

"Laurens?" I ask. "Yeah, she knew. Right before I killed her."

Mom blanches. "Harley."

"Arthur, Jimmy, Vince, all of them are gone, Mom. No one's left that can hurt you now."

"Harley." She reaches for me, but I pull away.

"I can't," I whisper, moving to Zack.

"You need me?" he asks, keeping his eyes on my mother.

"No." I shake my head. "I think we're done here." I get the glass of wine Zack poured earlier and gulp it down. "We can go."

"Harley. Please."

"No." I stop her from touching me. "I don't want to believe that you're a monster. I know you're not like them, but I don't know who you are, really. I can't pick everything apart to find the full truth here."

I grab Zack's hand.

"I'm done with this," I say and walk out of the kitchen.

Zack follows me through the living room and out the front door.

We walk down the steps, past the rose garden, to his car.

I climb into the passenger seat and wait for him to get in the driver's side.

"You're sure about this?" he asks as he turns the car on.

I grip my knees. "She had horrible decisions forced on her. She has to live every day remembering what she did, her part in all of this. And at the end of it, I grew up knowing she loved me. That's the truth I know. It's what I'm going to hold onto."

"Truth is truth, Harley. You don't have to choose to believe it, there is no choice."

"I have you." I look to him. "That's another truth."

He softens. "Yes. You do, little bird. You have me. Forever."

"All right, then." I smile. "Let's fly away. Together."

THIRTY FOUR

Zack

"Maybe they changed their minds." Harley paces in front of the door. It's cool today. The fall breeze runs right through my jacket.

"You should have worn a coat." I rub her arms through her sweater.

"I'm fine," she assures me, walking away and starting her pacing again.

"Are you nervous because we've been away for a while?" I question her. We've spent the last four months traveling. I've shown Harley every one of my five houses, and introduced her to those who will keep us safe during our hunts.

She didn't hesitate when I explained she was welcome to join in my endeavors. Slaying monsters keeps her mind quiet.

"No. I'm fine with that." She checks her phone. "Do you think it would be safe to stop at the cemetery before we leave?"

"Of course. We have nothing to worry about. The FBI wrote off Agent Laurens murder as a mob hit. Jimmy Blackwood is still missing, and considering he killed an FBI agent, his family is just fine with him being gone."

There's been no backlash from Jacob Blackwood. Turns out, he was unaware of his cousin's side business. And being a man with a sliver of a soul, he couldn't find it in him to seek retribution for his cousin.

Especially when evidence was sent to him that Jimmy had trafficked a classmate of Jacob's daughter.

"Your mom?" I ask when her phone vibrates in her hand.

She frowns. "Yeah. I told her we'd be in town." They've been talking a little, here and there, over the last few weeks. "Mom is going to meet us at the cemetery if that's okay with you?"

I hug her to me when a chilly wind blows.

"Of course it is, little bird." I kiss the top of her head. "If you're up for it."

She nods, my chin getting hit by the top of her head.

"A short visit." It won't last a second longer than will make her comfortable.

The clean-up crew found boxes of old videos stashed in the mechanic's shop. In one of them was her mother. I don't tell my girl 'no' very often, but I didn't let her put eyes on that video. It was enough that I watched the hell her mother went through. I gave her the PG-13 version so she could let her mind rest that her mother had told her the truth.

Nancy can't make up for the horrors of the past, but maybe, one day they'll be able to get back to a place where Harley trusts her again.

I'm not holding my breath, but if it gives Harley hope, then I'm all for it.

"See. Here they are." I pat her back.

A car pulls off the main road onto the gravel drive, heading toward us.

We watch as the Jeep Wrangler parks in front of where we stand. Charlie, Jackie, and Sharon climb out of the Jeep. Casper steps out of the driver's side.

"Hey." Charlie hugs Harley first. "Thanks for being here."

"Of course." Harley smiles. "Are you sure you're ready for this?"

"I've been ready for the last four months, but Casper said I had to wait." She rolls her eyes. "He's a bit bossy, this guy."

The rose shaped ring on her finger suggests she's fine with the arrangement.

"Well, the wait's over." Casper brings three wooden baseball bats from the back of the Jeep and hands them out to the ladies.

"If you're ready, might as well get going. He pissed himself a little when he woke up and realized what was happening. So, ignore the smell." I unlock the steel door of the industrial storage unit.

I peek inside.

Steven stands on his tip toes, his hands bound overhead where he dangles from a hook. He's just low enough that his toes brush the ground. But when they get started, he'll swing.

Charlie looks at her sister and then her mother.

"Ready?"

Sharon nods.

Jackie checks her grip on the bat. "Fuck, yes."

"All right, let's go." Charlie's the first one in, charging, leading the way.

The bat already in motion.

If you loved Marked and want more vigilante serial killer romance, check out Dolly.

ABOUT MEASHA STONE

Measha Stone is a USA Today bestselling romance author with a deep love for romantic stories, specifically those involving the darker side of romance, all the possessive dominant heroes, and their feisty heroines. If you love a well deserved happily ever after, you will enjoy her books.

https://www.meashastone.com

ALSO BY MEASHA STONE

EVER AFTER
Beast

Tower

Red

Hound

Siren

GIRLS OF THE ANNEX
Daddy Ever After

Obediently Ever After

DARK LACE SERIES
Club Dark Lace (Boxset)

Unzoned

Until Daddy

DARK ROMANCE STANDALONES
Valor

Kristoff

Dolly

Finding His Strength

Simmer

The Mob Boss' Pet

Gray

OWNED AND PROTECTED

Protecting His Pet

Protecting His Runaway

His Captive Pet

His Captive Kitten

Becoming His Pet

Training His Pet

MAFIA BRIDES

(Staszek Family)

Taken By Him

Kept By Him

Captivated By Him

RELUCTANT BRIDES

(Kaczmarek Family)

Unwilling Pawn

Reluctant Surrender

Veiled Treasure

INNOCENT BRIDES

Corrupted Innocence

Ruined Innocence

Ravaged Innocence

Surrendered Innocence

Savored Innocence

SACRED OBSESSION

Sacred Vow

Solemn Vow

Unbreakable Vow

BLACK LIGHT SERIES

Black Light Valentine Roulette

Black Light Cuffed

Black Light Roulette Redux

Black Light Suspicion

Black Light Celebrity Roulette

Black Light Roulette War

Black Light Roulette Rematch

Windy City SERIES

Hidden Heart

Secured Heart

Indebted Heart

Liberated Heart

Daddy's Heart

Windy City Box Set